Artful Deception

The Past Whispers through Every Falling Leaf

A Tumblebrook Mystery
Book 1

Ellen Le Teace

Bradford Press

Chapter 1

Whispers of Autumn

Golden rays of early autumn sunlight spilled over the North Shore town of Tumblebrook, painting the village in hues of amber and rust. The crisp air carried the faint aroma of pumpkin spice and freshly baked pies, mingling with bursts of laughter from workers setting up for the Fall Festival.

Amelia Farnsworth, owner of The Lakeside Inn, stood on the wide front porch of her establishment, clipboard in hand, surveying the hustle and bustle. The inn's shingled roof and white-trimmed windows gleamed against the backdrop of a cerulean lake, the very picture of small-town charm. A quiet satisfaction stirred in her chest, tempered by the familiar flutter of festival-day nerves.

"Clara, did the cider arrive?" Amelia called, her voice carrying a blend of authority and warmth. Her auburn hair was swept into a neat bun, and her well-worn cardigan hung loosely over her shoulders, giving her the air of someone who thrived on orchestrating organized chaos.

Clara emerged from the kitchen, brushing flour off her apron. "It's here, along with more pumpkins than we'll know what to do with," she said briskly, adjusting her glasses before handing Amelia a slip of paper. "I checked off everything, except the hay bales. They're late again."

Amelia sighed, tucking a loose strand of hair behind her ear. "Of course they are. What's a festival without a last-minute crisis?"

The Lakeside Inn was the heart of Tumblebrook, especially during the annual Fall Festival. For weeks, the town transformed into an autumnal wonderland, attracting visitors from near and far. Amelia thrived on the sense of community it fostered, even if it meant juggling endless details and a revolving door of guests. Yet, this year, an unshakable sense of unease lingered beneath the festival's cheer, whispering at the edges of her thoughts.

She glanced at the list before tucking it into her pocket. "I'll deal with the hay bales. Could you keep an eye on things here?"

Clara nodded, her no-nonsense demeanor a reassuring steadiness. "No problem. Lady Grey's been prowling the kitchen again. You might want to check on her before she starts reorganizing your spice rack."

Amelia smiled. Lady Grey, her British Shorthair cat, had an uncanny knack for meddling in ways that were equal parts inconvenient and endearing. "I'll look in on her after I—" Her words cut off as a black sedan rolled up the inn's gravel driveway.

A tall man with silver-threaded hair and a tweed blazer stepped out, exuding casual sophistication. He paused to take in his surroundings before climbing the porch steps.

"Dr. Westwood, I presume?" Amelia greeted him, extending her hand with a practiced smile.

He returned the gesture, his handshake firm. "You must be Ms. Farnsworth. It's a pleasure to meet you. This place is even more charming than I imagined."

"Thank you. We do our best to live up to expectations," she replied. "I trust your trip wasn't too tiring?"

"Not at all. The drive was rather scenic," he said, his British accent adding a refined lilt to his words. "I've been looking forward to this festival. There's nothing quite like the traditions of a small town to lend authenticity to one's research."

Amelia's brow lifted slightly. "Research?"

"Ah, yes. I'm a criminologist by trade, but folklore and community dynamics are a personal interest of mine." His gaze wandered to the banners and booths being set up in the distance. "Tumblebrook's reputation precedes it."

Before Amelia could respond, a loud argument drew their attention toward the town square. Two figures stood in heated discussion near a booth adorned with wrought-iron sculptures. One was Gregor Steele, the town's coppersmith and an artist renowned for his intricate metalwork. Opposite him was Edith Cranston, a no-nonsense council member known for her stubbornness.

Amelia frowned. "What's it about this time?"

"Something to do with the placement of his display. Gregor claims the new spot doesn't suit his work, and Edith insists there's no room to move it," Clara said dryly. "She's probably right, but you know Gregor. He won't back down."

Dr. Westwood observed the scene thoughtfully. "Quite the character. Does he often find himself at odds with the town council?"

"Often enough," Amelia admitted. "But Gregor's harmless. Stubborn, sure, but his heart's in the right place. Edith, on the other hand, is... well, particular about how things should run."

The argument ended with Gregor throwing up his hands and stomping away, muttering under his breath. Edith remained by the booth, arms crossed, and lips pressed into a thin line.

"A clash of wills, it seems," Dr. Westwood remarked neutrally.

"Typical festival drama," Amelia said with a sigh. "It'll blow over by tomorrow." She hoped her words would prove true, but the unease she'd felt earlier now hummed louder.

As the day wore on, preparations continued smoothly. Guests began arriving, filling the inn with the cheerful buzz of conversation. Amelia checked in visitors, directed staff, and ensured everything ran like clockwork. By late afternoon, the inn's kitchen brimmed with the comforting aroma of Clara's pumpkin bread, and twilight painted the sky in streaks of pink and orange.

Lady Grey appeared then, padding into the common room with deliberate steps. Her amber eyes were alert and inquisitive, and she carried something in her mouth.

"What have you got there, Lady?" Amelia crouched to inspect her feline companion.

Lady Grey dropped the object at Amelia's feet: a paintbrush, its bristles flecked with dried blue paint.

"Where did you find this?" Amelia picked up the brush, examining it closely. It wasn't one she recognized from the inn.

Dr. Westwood, who had been browsing a bookshelf, looked up with interest. "A clue, perhaps?" he teased.

"A clue to what?" Amelia laughed, though curiosity tinged her amusement. Lady Grey stared up at her, tail swishing, as if expecting something more.

"Cats are remarkably perceptive creatures," Dr. Westwood said. "She may have stumbled upon something worth investigating."

Amelia pocketed the paintbrush, resolving to ask around during the festival. For now, it was just another oddity in a day full of them.

As dusk settled over Tumblebrook, the town square came alive with twinkling fairy lights and the murmur of excitement. Amelia stood near the inn's entrance, watching the scene unfold. Despite the occasional hiccups, the festival was shaping up to be as magical as ever. Still, the paintbrush in her pocket and the earlier argument between Gregor and Edith lingered in her mind like unfinished thoughts.

Lady Grey brushed against her leg, purring softly. Amelia scratched behind her ears, finding comfort in the familiar rhythm. Whatever tomorrow brought, she knew one thing for certain: Tumblebrook was never short on surprises.

The festivities continued to swell, the air thick with the smells of roasted chestnuts and cinnamon. Families bustled through the stalls, children giggling as they dragged their parents toward the caramel apple stand. Amid the joviality, Amelia's gaze drifted back to Gregor. He stood at the edge of the square, speaking in hushed tones to a woman Amelia didn't immediately recognize. The brim of her felt hat obscured her face, but her tense posture suggested something serious.

"Who's that?" Amelia murmured, more to herself than anyone else.

Dr. Westwood appeared at her side, following her gaze. "Interesting. Gregor doesn't strike me as someone prone to clandestine meetings."

"No, he doesn't," Amelia agreed. She was about to step closer when the woman turned abruptly, striding off toward the darker end of the square where the streetlights barely reached.

Gregor stood motionless for a moment, then stalked off in the opposite direction, his shoulders rigid. Amelia couldn't shake the feeling she'd just witnessed something significant.

That night, Lady Grey settled herself on the front desk, her amber eyes following Amelia's every move as if to say, *Pay attention. You're missing something.*

Amelia sighed and patted the cat's head. "All right, Lady. Tomorrow, we'll see what you've dragged us into."

The paintbrush in her pocket felt heavier as she climbed the stairs. Upstairs, Lady Grey had already claimed her spot on Amelia's bed, her steady purring filling the room. Amelia pulled the paintbrush from her pocket, holding it up to the dim light of her bedside lamp. The dried blue paint glinted faintly, almost mocking in its simplicity.

It was just a brush—or was it?

Amelia placed it on her nightstand with a sigh. "We'll figure this out tomorrow," she said aloud, as if to convince herself. Lady Grey's tail flicked in response, and Amelia couldn't help but smile. Whatever mystery lay ahead, she wouldn't face it alone.

Chapter 2

A Painter's Fall

The morning sun struggled to pierce the thick clouds rolling in from the lake, casting Tumblebrook in a muted gray light. Dr. Jonathan Westwood adjusted his scarf against the brisk wind as he strolled toward the square. His curiosity about small-town dynamics had drawn him to Tumblebrook, but the undercurrent of tension he'd observed the day before lingered in his mind. The disagreement between Gregor Steele and Edith Cranston replayed vividly—an argument simmering with more than artistic pride.

As he neared the wrought-iron booth Gregor had painstakingly set up the previous day, an unease settled over him. The square was unnervingly quiet for a festival morning. The laughter and chatter that had animated the streets last night were gone, replaced by an eerie stillness.

Jonathan's eyes fell on the booth, and his breath caught. Gregor Steele lay sprawled on the cobblestones beside it, his body unnaturally twisted. A single overturned paintbox lay nearby, its contents scattered haphazardly.

"Good heavens," Jonathan muttered, hurrying forward. He crouched beside the body, his trained eye quickly assessing the scene.

Gregor's face was ashen, his lips tinged with blue. A faint metallic scent hung in the air, mingling with the damp tang of rain-soaked earth.

Jonathan couldn't help but recall the passion and precision Gregor poured into his work. Each wrought-iron sculpture was brimming with life, meticulously designed as if every curve and detail carried meaning. Gregor's creations were more than art—they were a statement of identity. By contrast, Edith Cranston had exuded sharp pragmatism the day before, her clipped tone and calculated demeanor leaving little room for sentimentality. The memory of their clash sharpened in Jonathan's mind.

"This isn't just about placement, Edith!" Gregor's voice had boomed across the square, frustration evident in every word. "You're undermining the entire purpose of this festival!"

Edith, unfazed, had replied coldly, "The festival is about the community, Gregor, not your personal gallery. Everyone's contributions deserve equal prominence."

Even then, Jonathan had sensed the dispute was about more than logistics. There had been history between the two—a tension laced with resentment. Gregor's trembling hands and his thick voice betrayed emotion far deeper than annoyance. *You don't understand what these pieces represent. You never have,* he'd said.

Edith's sharp retort had cut through the air. "And perhaps that's the problem. You think they matter more than they do."

Now, standing over Gregor's lifeless body, Jonathan felt the weight of that argument anew. What had Edith meant by her dismissal? And why had Gregor reacted so viscerally? These sculptures, twisted and intricate, seemed to hum with unspoken meaning. One depicted a bird mid-flight, its outstretched wings rendered with astonishing detail. Another was a gnarled tree, its branches brimming with sorrow and resilience. They weren't just decorative pieces—they were stories carved into iron.

"Dr. Westwood!"

Jonathan turned to see Amelia Farnsworth rushing toward him, her cardigan flapping in the wind. Her auburn hair, usually pinned neatly, was tousled, and her expression blended shock with alarm. Clara followed close behind, apron hastily removed and clutched in her hands.

"Is that—" Amelia's voice faltered as she stopped short, her wide eyes locking onto Gregor. "Oh no."

Jonathan rose, keeping his tone calm and steady. "It appears Gregor's had an accident. Though I'm not entirely convinced it's just that."

Amelia's hand flew to her mouth. "You think it might be foul play?"

"I'm not ruling it out," Jonathan said grimly. "The position of his body... it's odd. And the paintbox—"

"You're thinking about their argument, aren't you?" Amelia interrupted.

He nodded. "This wasn't just about placement. Gregor's reaction yesterday was... intense. Almost desperate."

"Desperate?" Amelia frowned.

Jonathan glanced back at the sculptures. "It's as if he believed these held some kind of truth or significance that Edith didn't want to acknowledge."

Clara, who had been listening quietly, spoke up. "Gregor was like that with all his work. He once told me his art was a way of preserving what others wanted to forget."

Jonathan's brows lifted. "Preserving what?"

Clara hesitated. "He didn't elaborate. But I got the sense he meant history... or secrets."

Jonathan turned his attention to the wrought-iron pieces again. "If his art was preserving secrets, perhaps Edith's dismissal wasn't just about pride. If she wanted something forgotten, Gregor's work would have been a threat."

Amelia crossed her arms, deep in thought. "But what could she want forgotten? Edith isn't the sentimental type. She's practical to a fault."

"Practicality can be a mask," Jonathan said. "Sometimes, a person's efforts to suppress something say more than the secret itself."

Clara stepped closer to the booth; her gaze fixed on the sculptures. "If these pieces are the key, then maybe the answer lies in the work itself."

Jonathan nodded. "Agreed. But we'll need to examine them carefully. If Gregor hid meaning in these, it won't be obvious."

He crouched again, this time examining the paintbrushes and scattered paint tubes near the overturned box. "Notice how these brushes are arranged—almost like a pattern. And this..." He reached for a small piece of paper partially tucked beneath a cobalt blue tube. The writing was smudged but still legible: *To know the truth, follow the path of shadows.*

Amelia read over his shoulder, her brow furrowing. "What could that mean?"

"It's cryptic, certainly," Jonathan said, standing. "But it suggests Gregor was onto something. Or that someone wanted us to think he was."

The conversation halted as Lady Grey padded purposefully into the square, her sleek gray coat shimmering faintly in the dim light. Her amber eyes glinted with an almost knowing intensity.

Amelia crouched to meet her. "What is it, Lady?" The cat sniffed the air before circling the paintbox, her tail swishing. "She's onto something," Amelia murmured.

Lady Grey stopped beside Gregor's outstretched hand, pawing gently at the fingers before letting out a soft meow. Jonathan crouched down and carefully moved the hand aside, revealing a small, folded note. "Good work, Lady Grey," he said, unfolding the damp paper.

The message was faint but clear: *Mine... secrets buried.*

Clara's voice was a whisper. "The mine again. That place has been closed for years. No one goes there anymore."

"This can't be a coincidence," Amelia said. "Sheriff Bell is on his way. He'll want to see this."

When Sheriff Bell arrived, his face was a mask of stern focus. Jonathan relayed their observations as the sheriff surveyed the scene.

"This note," Bell said, holding up the damp paper. "You're sure it was here?"

"Positive," Jonathan replied. "There's also this: a second note points us to the mine."

Bell's expression darkened. "No one's leaving town until we get to the bottom of this. If it's foul play, I'll have answers."

Amelia felt a chill run through her as Lady Grey leapt onto the booth, batting at a sculpture until another folded note fell to the ground. Clara picked it up and read aloud: *Beware the false light.*

Jonathan's brow furrowed. "False light? What could that mean?"

Bell's jaw tightened. "It means this just got a whole lot more complicated."

Amelia scooped up Lady Grey, who purred softly against her shoulder. Whispering, she said, "Good girl. You're always one step ahead, aren't you?"

Jonathan met her gaze, his tone steady. "One step ahead indeed. Let's hope we can keep up."

Chapter 3

Storms of the Past

The day dawned crisp and golden, but Amelia Farnsworth's mood matched the heavy clouds creeping over Tumble-brook. She stood in the kitchen of The Lakeside Inn, her hands buried in a mound of dough she was kneading for breakfast scones. The rhythmic motion, usually soothing, did little to calm her restless thoughts. The discovery of Gregor Steele's body had sent shockwaves through the town, but Amelia couldn't shake the feeling that something far more sinister lurked beneath the surface.

"Clara, can you check on the tea water?" she called over her shoulder, glancing at the clock. Guests would be coming down for breakfast any moment, and everything needed to be perfect—even if her thoughts were far from it.

Clara, ever efficient, bustled to the kettle. "Already on it. Have you seen Lady Grey? She's usually underfoot by now."

Amelia wiped her hands on her apron and frowned. "Not since last night. She's probably out inspecting something. You know how she is when there's a mystery afoot."

Clara smirked faintly. "She's as curious as her owner."

Amelia didn't reply, her mind drifting back to the cryptic notes found near Gregor's body. The words lingered like smoke in her thoughts: *To know the truth, follow the path of shadows.* What shadows? And why did everything seem to point to that abandoned mine?

The first guests began trickling into the dining room, their cheerful chatter filling the air. Amelia greeted each of them with a practiced smile, serving coffee and scones while fielding compliments about Clara's pumpkin bread. Outwardly, everything ran smoothly, but inwardly, Amelia was elsewhere, her thoughts flitting between fragments of unanswered questions.

By mid-morning, the dining room had cleared, leaving Amelia a rare moment of quiet. As she tidied up, Lady Grey made her entrance, leaping gracefully onto a windowsill. The cat's tail flicked; her amber eyes locked on Amelia with an expression that could only be described as knowing.

"There you are," Amelia said, scratching behind the cat's ears. "Find anything interesting on your travels?"

Lady Grey purred, but her gaze darted to the corner of the room, where a stack of old newspapers sat on a side table. Amelia followed her line of sight and frowned. "What is it, girl?"

The cat hopped down, padding to the table. She batted at the stack with her paw until one of the papers slid free. Intrigued, Amelia picked it up. It wasn't a current issue—it was a yellowed edition of the *Tumblebrook Gazette* from nearly a decade ago. Her eyes caught the headline: *Dispute Over Mine Rights Escalates.*

Her heart skipped a beat. The article detailed a conflict between local artisans and a development company intent on reopening the mine. Gregor Steele's name appeared several times, alongside Edith Cranston's. According to the piece, Gregor had been one of the most vocal opponents, while Edith had initially supported the project before abruptly changing her stance.

Amelia pulled up a chair, reading the article carefully. The proposed project aimed to revitalize the abandoned mine as a source of raw materials for commercial use. While some residents had championed the potential economic benefits, others—Gregor chief among them—had protested vehemently, citing environmental risks and the loss of the town's artisanal heritage.

Gregor's quotes were fiery: *"This mine represents the soul of Tumblebrook. Turning it into a factory for outsiders to exploit is a betrayal of everything we stand for."*

Edith, in contrast, had been pragmatic: *"We need to think about the future of our town. Reopening the mine could provide jobs and resources we desperately need."*

But as Amelia read further, she noted a shift. After a contentious town meeting, Edith had reversed her position, joining the opposition. Her reasoning was vague, citing a "change of heart" and a renewed "understanding of the community's values."

"Change of heart, my foot," Amelia muttered. Edith Cranston wasn't known for sentimentality, and her sudden reversal reeked of ulterior motives.

Lady Grey meowed softly, breaking Amelia's focus. The cat pawed at the stack of newspapers again, drawing Amelia's attention to another edition. Flipping through its pages, she found follow-up articles documenting the development company's abrupt withdrawal. One hinted at veiled threats against the company's representatives, though no specifics were provided.

A small sidebar caught her eye—a reporter's speculative editorial: *The company's withdrawal may not be as simple as public pressure. Rumors persist of undisclosed discoveries within the mine that could complicate its reopening.*

Amelia leaned back in her chair, her mind racing. What discoveries could have been buried in that mine? Why had Gregor fought so hard to protect it, even as Edith's stance shifted? The threads of the past tangled together, but Amelia couldn't shake the feeling that the answers to Gregor's death lay somewhere in that abandoned shaft.

"Curious," she murmured. "What were you trying to show me, Lady?"

The cat meowed again, hopping back onto the table. She pawed at a folded piece of paper wedged between the newspapers. Amelia unfolded it carefully, her breath catching as she read the handwritten note:

If the truth comes to light, it will ruin us all. Burn this.

The signature was missing, but the handwriting was sharp and angular, and it sparked a twinge of recognition. Her pulse quickened. Could this note be connected to Gregor's death? And if so, who had wanted it destroyed?

* * *

Later that afternoon, Amelia found herself in the crowded town hall for the emergency meeting called by Sheriff Bell. The room buzzed with hushed conversations as residents filled the rows of chairs. Taking a seat near the back, Amelia glanced at Clara, who sat beside her, notebook in hand, her sharp eyes scanning the room.

Sheriff Bell raised a hand for silence, his presence commanding. "Thank you all for coming," he began, his deep voice cutting through the murmurs. "I'll keep this brief. As many of you know, Gregor Steele was found dead yesterday morning. While we're still waiting on the medical examiner's report, the circumstances are suspicious. Until we know more, I'm asking everyone to remain vigilant and report anything unusual."

A hand shot up in the middle of the room. Edith Cranston stood, her expression tight. "Sheriff, are you suggesting foul play?"

Bell's gaze didn't waver. "I'm not ruling it out."

Unease rippled through the crowd. Edith sat down, her eyes darting briefly toward Amelia. The flicker of something—guilt? Defiance?—crossed her face before she looked away.

Another hand went up. Henry Swinton, who ran a food stall at the festival, cleared his throat. "Sheriff, I saw Gregor arguing with someone the day before—not just Edith. He was talking to that vendor selling handmade jewelry. It didn't look friendly."

Bell's eyes narrowed. "The jeweler? Name?"

"Samantha Reed," Henry said. "She's new to the festival, but I've seen her around town a few times."

Bell nodded. "We'll follow up. Anyone else?"

Muted murmurs filled the room, but no other hands went up. Amelia sensed the underlying tension in the crowd. Tumblebrook thrived on its close-knit community, but the shadow of Gregor's death was unraveling their trust.

"One more thing," Bell said. "I've heard rumors about the abandoned mine and its connection to Gregor. Let me be clear—the mine is off-limits. It's unsafe, and anyone found trespassing will be dealt with accordingly."

Amelia's brow furrowed. Bell's warning only deepened her suspicions. What about the mine tied all this together?

As the meeting adjourned, Amelia lingered near the back, catching snippets of whispered conversations.

"Do you think it's about the mine? There's always been something strange about that place."

"Gregor always made enemies when he spoke his mind."

"Edith knows more than she's saying..."

Clara joined her. "You're thinking about the mine, aren't you?" she asked quietly.

Amelia nodded. "It keeps coming up. Gregor's notes, the articles, Bell's warning... There's more to this than anyone's letting on."

Back at the inn, Lady Grey greeted them at the door, twining around Amelia's legs before darting toward the parlor. Amelia followed to find the cat perched beside a small leather-bound journal on the coffee table. The initials G.S. were embossed on the cover.

"Gregor Steele," Clara murmured. "Where did this come from?"

Amelia opened it, her breath catching at Gregor's deliberate handwriting. Each entry chronicled his suspicions about the mine— missing shipments, whispered threats, and secrets buried beneath the surface. One chilling note in the margins read:

They think the past is buried, but it's alive, waiting. If anything happens to me, start with Edith.

Amelia looked up, her resolve hardening. "This journal... it's a map to everything Gregor feared. And it all leads back to the mine."

Clara nodded. "What do we do now?"

Amelia glanced at Lady Grey, whose amber eyes gleamed with quiet determination. "We follow the shadows," she said softly. "And we start with Edith."

Chapter 4

Canvas Secrets

Clara adjusted her glasses as she carefully spread the faded piece of canvas across the wooden work table in her bookstore. Morning light streamed through the large bay window, illuminating the delicate fibers of the mysterious fragment. It was stained in places, its once-vibrant colors muted by time and neglect, but the intricate design—a swirling mix of blues and golds— hinted at something extraordinary.

She had always been drawn to puzzles, and this scrap of canvas, tucked in the pages of Gregor Steele's journal, was no exception. Its presence raised more questions than answers, and Clara was determined to uncover its secrets.

"Do you think it's from one of Gregor's works?" Amelia's voice pulled Clara from her thoughts. Amelia stood nearby; Lady Grey perched on her shoulder like a vigilant sentinel.

"Possibly," Clara replied, running her fingers gently over the edge of the canvas. "But the texture and brushstrokes don't match his typical style. Gregor's ironwork was precise, almost mechanical, but this... this is chaotic. Passionate."

Dr. Westwood leaned in, his keen eyes studying the fragment. "It almost looks deliberate, like it's part of a larger piece. Could it have been cut from a painting?"

Clara nodded thoughtfully. "That's what I'm thinking. It's too intricate to be random. Whoever painted this was talented. But why would Gregor hide it in his journal?"

Amelia set Lady Grey down, the cat landing gracefully before padding over to the table. "If it's not Gregor's work, whose could it be?"

Clara hesitated, her analytical mind already piecing together a theory. "There were rumors... years ago, about a gallery theft in Tumblebrook. Several paintings disappeared, and they were never recovered."

Dr. Westwood's brow furrowed. "You think this fragment could be connected?"

"It's possible," Clara said, retrieving a magnifying glass from her desk drawer. She examined the canvas closely, her sharp eyes catching something faint near the corner. "There's a mark here. It's hard to make out, but it looks like a signature."

Amelia leaned closer; her curiosity piqued. "Can you identify it?"

Clara adjusted the glass, angling it toward the light. "It's partially faded, but it's definitely an artist's signature. This could be a clue to its origin. If we figure out who painted this, it might lead us to the missing paintings—or to whoever wanted them hidden."

The fragment's texture was unusual, Clara realized as she scrutinized it further. Unlike typical canvases, this one seemed coarser, as though it had been salvaged or repurposed. Running her fingers along the edges, she noticed faint scorch marks.

"This piece was damaged at some point," Clara said aloud. "But look here." She pointed to a tiny indentation in the corner, a pressed insignia barely visible beneath the painted surface. "This is a gallery mark."

Dr. Westwood's eyes lit up. "A gallery mark? Are you sure?"

"Positive," Clara replied. "I've seen something similar in archival paintings. It's a way of cataloging works for exhibits. This fragment came from a significant piece—something worth protecting."

Amelia leaned forward, her gaze flickering between the fragment and Clara. "But why would Gregor have it? And why hide it in his journal?"

Clara's mind raced as she pieced together possibilities. "What if Gregor found the fragment while investigating something else? Maybe he thought it was connected to the mine. Or..." Her voice trailed off.

"Or?" Amelia prompted.

"Or he knew whoever created this painting," Clara said. "And he wanted to protect them."

Lady Grey let out a soft meow, her tail curling around her paws. She stared intently at the fragment, as if agreeing with Clara's hypothesis.

Later that afternoon, Clara's investigation led her to the town archives. Surrounded by stacks of brittle newspapers and dusty records, she searched for any mention of the missing gallery paintings. After an hour of fruitless digging, she finally found an article from over two decades ago. The headline read: *Gallery Heist Leaves Town Reeling.*

The article described a bold theft from the prestigious Tumblebrook Gallery, where several irreplaceable paintings had been stolen in the dead of night. One piece was highlighted—*The Veil of Shadows,* a haunting masterpiece by an artist named Elias Carradine. The article noted Carradine's penchant for embedding symbolic details within his works, making them highly sought-after by collectors.

Clara's heart raced as she read the description of the painting. It depicted a forest at dusk, with light filtering through the trees and shadowy figures barely visible in the background. The swirling blues and golds mentioned in the article matched the fragment's colors exactly.

She snapped a photo of the article with her phone and sent it to Amelia and Dr. Westwood, adding a brief message: *I think I know where the fragment came from. It's part of a stolen Carradine.*

Minutes later, Amelia called. "Clara, are you saying this fragment is from a painting stolen twenty years ago?"

"Exactly," Clara replied, her voice steady but tinged with excitement. "And not just any painting. *The Veil of Shadows* was the centerpiece of the heist. If this fragment survived, it means the rest of the painting might still be out there."

Dr. Westwood's voice cut in on the call. "If Gregor had this fragment, he must have stumbled onto something significant. We need to find out how he got it—and why it was hidden."

"I'll keep digging," Clara promised. "But we're dealing with a web of secrets that's been buried for decades."

That evening, the trio convened in the cozy sitting room of The Lakeside Inn. The canvas fragment was carefully stored in a protective sleeve, while Gregor's journal lay open on the coffee table. Determination to unravel the mystery united them.

"We need to find out more about this gallery theft," Dr. Westwood said. "If these paintings were stolen, there must be records—police reports, news articles, something we can trace."

Amelia nodded. "I'll reach out to Sheriff Bell. He might have access to the old case files."

Clara tapped her pen against her notebook. "I'll search the archives at the bookstore. If there's anything in the old newspapers, I'll find it."

Dr. Westwood stood; his expression resolute. "And I'll visit the local artists' collective. If anyone knows about these missing paintings, it'll be them."

Their plan set, the three dispersed. But as Amelia walked Dr. Westwood to the door, she noticed something unusual. Just beyond the porch, where the damp ground bore traces of morning dew, was a faint trail of footprints.

"Jonathan," she called, gesturing toward the marks. "Look at this."

He joined her, his eyes narrowing as he studied the trail. The prints led around the side of the inn toward the back garden. "These weren't here last night," he said. "And they don't match any of the guests' shoes."

Amelia's stomach tightened. "Do you think someone's been snooping around?"

Dr. Westwood nodded. "It's possible. Whoever it was didn't want to be seen."

Lady Grey, who had followed them onto the porch, let out a low growl, her ears flattening. She darted toward the garden, disappearing into the hedges.

"She's onto something," Amelia said, hurrying after her. Dr. Westwood followed; his curiosity piqued.

They found Lady Grey near the edge of the garden, pawing at a pile of overturned soil. Something glinted in the sunlight, partially buried beneath the dirt.

Amelia crouched down, brushing away the soil to reveal a small, tarnished key. She held it up, her mind racing. "A key? But to what?"

Dr. Westwood's expression darkened. "We'll need to find out. For now, keep it safe. Whoever left it might come back for it."

At the bookstore, as Clara sifted through the archives, her phone buzzed with a text from an unknown number: *Check the abandoned studio on Elm. You'll find what you're looking for.*

Her pulse quickened. Who would send such a cryptic message, and how did they know about her investigation? She hesitated, debating whether to involve Amelia and Dr. Westwood, but her curiosity got the better of her.

The studio, once owned by a reclusive artist who had disappeared years ago, was a shadow of its former self. Its windows were boarded up, and the paint on its exterior had long since peeled away. Clara approached cautiously, the key from the garden in her pocket. It fit the lock perfectly.

Inside, the air was thick with dust and the scent of turpentine. Paintings, some finished and others half-completed, leaned against the walls. But what caught Clara's eye was a large canvas draped with a tattered sheet. She pulled it away, revealing a painting that took her breath away.

It depicted the Tumblebrook mine, but not as it was now. The scene was alive with color, showing miners at work beneath a golden sunset. But there was something unsettling about it—a shadowy figure lingered in the background; its features obscured.

Clara snapped a photo and sent it to Amelia with a single message: *We need to talk. Now.*

Amelia received the photo just as the inn's kitchen was settling down for the night. Lady Grey hopped onto the counter and stared intently at the phone as if she, too, were examining the image.

"What do you see, Lady?" Amelia asked softly. The cat tilted her head, her tail flicking back and forth. Amelia studied the photo again. The shadowy figure in the painting seemed almost deliberate, as if the artist had hidden it on purpose. Was it symbolic, or something more literal?

The trio gathered at The Lakeside Inn to discuss their findings. Clara spread the fragment, the journal, and the article across the coffee table. Dr. Westwood examined the photo of *The Veil of Shadows*, his brow furrowed.

"Carradine's works were known for their symbolism," he said. "If this painting was stolen, there must have been a reason beyond its monetary value."

"Like what?" Amelia asked.

"Carradine was obsessed with hidden messages," Clara said. "His paintings often contained clues to real events or places. If *The Veil of*

Shadows had something to do with the mine, it could explain why someone wanted it erased from history."

Amelia's gaze shifted to Lady Grey, who was perched on the arm of the sofa, her amber eyes gleaming. "And Gregor must have known. That's why he had the fragment."

Dr. Westwood nodded. "But the question remains: who wants it hidden... and who's willing to kill to keep it that way?"

Lady Grey let out a low, insistent growl, her tail flicking sharply. Clara picked up the journal, running her fingers over its worn cover. The answers, she felt certain, were within their grasp. They just had to follow the path Carradine had painted—and the shadows Gregor had tried to illuminate.

Chapter 5

Through Lady Grey's Eyes

The sun had just begun to rise over Tumblebrook, casting a golden glow across the town. Amelia Farnsworth stood on the porch of The Lakeside Inn, a steaming cup of coffee in her hands. Despite the crisp beauty of the morning, her thoughts churned with the mysteries swirling around Gregor Steele, the abandoned mine, and the fragment of the stolen painting. She sipped her coffee, glancing down at Lady Grey, who perched elegantly on the porch railing, her tail flicking in contemplation.

"Well, my little detective, what's next?" Amelia asked with a faint smile. Lady Grey turned her amber eyes on her, as if to say, *Follow me.*

The cat leapt gracefully to the ground and padded toward the overgrown path leading to the old artist's studio. Amelia hesitated, glancing back at the inn. Clara was still asleep, and Dr. Westwood had planned a morning visit to the artists' collective. She wasn't entirely comfortable wandering off alone, but Lady Grey's purposeful movements convinced her to follow.

The studio stood at the edge of town, its weathered facade hidden behind a tangle of vines and brambles. Amelia had passed it countless times but never given it much thought. Now, as Lady Grey darted ahead and disappeared through a broken windowpane, she felt a twinge of unease.

"Wait for me, Lady," Amelia called, pushing open the creaking door. The scent of turpentine and mildew filled the air, mingling with the faint aroma of damp wood. Dust motes swirled in the sunlight filtering through cracked windows, illuminating a space that was equal parts chaotic and hauntingly beautiful.

Sketches were pinned haphazardly to the walls, their edges curling with age. Canvases—some blank, others bearing half-finished paintings—leaned against furniture that had seen better days. A battered easel stood in the center of the room, a palette of dried paint still resting on its surface. Amelia's gaze swept the room, noting the signs of abandonment—and of someone who had left in a hurry. Lady Grey sat atop an old trunk in the corner, her gaze fixed on Amelia.

"What have you found, girl?" Amelia asked, crossing the room. The trunk was locked, but the rusty clasp gave way with a bit of effort. Inside, she found a stack of journals, their covers faded and worn. The topmost journal bore the initials *E.C.*—Edith Cranston.

Amelia's breath caught. She opened the journal carefully, the pages filled with looping handwriting. It wasn't Gregor's—this was Edith's voice, raw and unfiltered. The entries spoke of her early years in Tumblebrook, her ambitions, and... her rivalry with Gregor Steele.

The journal revealed a web of complicated relationships. Edith and Gregor had once been close, bonded by their shared passion for art. But as their careers progressed, tensions grew. One entry described a heated argument over a gallery exhibition, with Gregor accusing Edith of sabotaging his chance at a major commission. Another hinted at a more personal connection—Edith's unrequited feelings for Gregor and her bitterness when he chose someone else.

"He's blind to what we could create together," Edith had written. "He's too caught up in his idealism, his obsession with legacy."

Amelia frowned, flipping through the pages. The entries grew darker, the handwriting more frantic. Edith's resentment had festered over the years, morphing into a cold determination to outshine Gregor. Yet there were also hints of regret, moments of vulnerability that painted her in a more sympathetic light.

"Legacy means nothing if it leaves only emptiness behind," Edith had scrawled in the margins of one page.

Lady Grey hopped gracefully onto a stack of books near a rickety desk in the corner. The desk was strewn with papers, brushes, and an old, cracked mirror that reflected Amelia's face as she approached. Faint red paint scrawled across the mirror read: *The truth lies beneath.*

"What on earth?" Amelia murmured, running her fingers across the words. The paint had dried long ago, but the message felt heavy with meaning.

Her eyes were drawn to the floorboards near the desk, where Lady Grey pawed insistently. Amelia knelt, brushing aside a thin layer of dust to reveal a faint seam in the wood. Her heart quickened as she pushed against the panel, which gave way with surprising ease, revealing a hidden compartment.

Inside was a small cloth-bound journal, its edges worn from years of handling. Amelia opened it carefully, her breath catching as she read the first page: *To those who seek the light, beware the shadows it casts.*

The handwriting was bold and confident, unmistakably Gregor's. She flipped through the pages, finding sketches, diagrams, and cryptic phrases interspersed with detailed accounts of his work—and his growing suspicions about the mine and its connection to the art community.

"This is incredible," Amelia whispered. "It's like a roadmap to everything he was trying to uncover."

She carried the journal to the easel, where a partially completed painting still stood. The work depicted a familiar scene: the entrance to the Tumblebrook mine. But unlike Gregor's serene landscapes, this painting was dark and foreboding, with shadowy figures lurking just beyond the entrance. The strokes were frantic, almost chaotic, as if he had painted it in a fevered state.

"What were you trying to tell us, Gregor?" Amelia wondered aloud.

Lady Grey let out a soft meow, drawing Amelia's attention to another corner of the studio. A stack of rolled-up canvases leaned against the wall, bound with twine. Amelia untied one and unrolled it carefully, revealing a vivid painting of a group of people gathered around a table. Their faces were familiar—Edith Cranston, Sheriff Bell, and even Gregor himself. But another figure stood in the background, their features obscured.

The painting's title was scrawled in the corner: *The Pact.*

Amelia's stomach churned. "A pact? What kind of pact?" She traced her fingers over the faces, her mind racing. The figure in the background—were they pulling the strings? Or had Gregor imagined them?

Amelia spent another hour in the studio, cataloging what she could. In addition to the journal and the paintings, she found a set of letters tucked into a drawer in the desk. These were different from the threatening notes she'd discovered earlier. They were addressed to Gregor, but the tone was pleading, almost desperate:

You think you've escaped the past, but it will catch up to you. The mine... the painting... it's all connected.

You're in too deep. Let it go before it's too late.

The mine isn't what you think. Stay away.

The letters were unsigned, but Amelia's instincts told her they had come from someone who had once cared for Gregor deeply. She tucked them into her bag along with the journal and paintings, her resolve hardening. Whatever Gregor had uncovered, it had cost him his life. But Amelia was determined to see his work through—and to uncover the truth, no matter where it led.

Lady Grey hopped onto her shoulder as she closed the studio door behind her. The cat's purr vibrated against Amelia's ear, a reassuring presence as they walked back toward the inn.

"Good work, Lady," Amelia said softly. "We're getting closer."

Amelia returned to the inn, her arms laden with the journals and letters. She spread them out on the dining room table, calling Clara and Dr. Westwood to join her. Lady Grey hopped onto a chair, curling her tail around her paws as if settling in for a long discussion.

"What have you got?" Clara asked, rubbing sleep from her eyes.

Amelia held up the journal. "Edith Cranston's personal journal. It details her rivalry with Gregor... and something more. She had feelings for him once, but their relationship soured over time. And look at these." She passed Clara the letters. "They're addressed to Gregor. The handwriting matches the note we found near his body."

Dr. Westwood examined the letters, his expression growing grim. "Whoever wrote these was deeply involved in whatever Gregor was trying to uncover. They mention the mine and the painting specifically."

"And Edith?" Clara asked, flipping through the journal.

"She's hiding something," Amelia said. "Her entries are full of anger and regret, but there's a moment where she mentions the council. She says, 'The council's vote was a farce. They knew about the mine, but they chose silence.'"

"The council?" Dr. Westwood's brows lifted. "You think they're involved?"

Amelia nodded. "Edith was part of the council for years. If there's a connection between the mine and the painting, the council may have been trying to cover it up."

Clara's eyes narrowed. "It makes sense. The council would have had the power to suppress information about the mine, especially if it threatened their interests."

Lady Grey let out a soft growl, her gaze fixed on the journal. Amelia stroked the cat's fur absently, her mind racing. They had pieces of the puzzle, but the picture was still incomplete.

* * *

That evening, Amelia and Dr. Westwood paid a visit to Edith Cranston. The former councilwoman lived in a stately home at the edge of town, her garden meticulously maintained. Edith greeted them with a polite but wary smile, her sharp eyes taking in their expressions.

"To what do I owe this visit?" she asked, leading them into her parlor.

Amelia hesitated, glancing at Dr. Westwood. "We've been looking into Gregor's death," she said finally. "And we found some things... in the old artist's studio."

Edith's smile faltered. "The studio? It's been abandoned for years."

"We found your journal," Dr. Westwood said bluntly. "And letters addressed to Gregor. Letters that suggest a connection between the mine, the painting, and... the council."

For a moment, Edith said nothing. Then she sighed, sinking into a chair. "You don't understand what you're digging into," she said. "The mine... it's not just a mine. And the council... we made choices to protect this town. Choices that weren't easy."

"Protect it from what?" Amelia pressed.

Edith's gaze hardened. "From the past. From secrets that should have stayed buried."

"Secrets like *The Veil of Shadows?*" Amelia asked, her voice firm.

Edith froze, her fingers tightening on the armrest. "You've seen it?"

"Not the full painting," Dr. Westwood said. "But we have a fragment. And it's enough to raise questions about what the council knew and why they acted as they did."

Edith's shoulders slumped. "It's more than you think," she said quietly. "The painting... the mine... they're intertwined. Carradine's work revealed truths about this town that some would kill to keep hidden."

Lady Grey, who had followed Amelia and Dr. Westwood into the room, leapt onto the sofa beside Edith, her amber eyes gleaming with intensity. Edith let out a bitter laugh, stroking the cat's fur. "Even she knows," Edith murmured. "The shadows are stirring."

Amelia's pulse quickened. They were on the verge of uncovering something monumental. But as Edith's words sank in, a chilling realization crept over her: whatever lay in the shadows might not be ready to let go of its secrets.

Chapter 6

Brushstrokes in Time

D r. Jonathan Westwood sat at the dining table in The Lakeside Inn, his gaze locked on Gregor Steele's journal. The inn's comforting warmth seemed to dissipate with each brittle page he turned. Intricate sketches, scattered notes, and enigmatic phrases demanded his full attention. To his left, Clara carefully copied diagrams into a notepad, her lips pressed in concentration, while Amelia moved briskly about with the tea service—a physical outlet for her restless thoughts.

Lady Grey, poised on the table's edge, was the only one at ease. Her luminous amber eyes tracked Jonathan's hand as it traced one of Gregor's diagrams, her tail flicking occasionally, as though silently weighing their progress.

"These markings here," Jonathan said, tapping a sketch of the town's layout, "they're not random. Gregor must have had a reason for marking these locations."

Clara leaned over, narrowing her eyes. "That's the old copper-smith shop, isn't it? And... this one is near the library."

"Yes," Jonathan said, tracing the faint lines. "And this..." He pointed to a circle sketched at the map's edge. "This is the mine entrance."

Amelia set a tray of tea on the table, her brow furrowing. "Do you think he was trying to find something?"

"Not just find," Jonathan replied, his tone measured. "Protect. These markings suggest caches. Look at this." He turned the journal toward Amelia and Clara, pointing to a note scrawled in the margin: *Each brushstroke hides a story. Protect what you can, for the light will not always shine.*

"What does that even mean?" Clara asked, her expression puzzled.

"It's symbolic," Jonathan said, leaning back thoughtfully. "But also, practical. If Gregor believed something important was hidden in these locations, we need to investigate."

Amelia's lips tightened. "The mine seems central to all of this, but we can't overlook the other places. Clara, can you investigate the library's records?"

Clara nodded, already jotting a list. "I'll start there."

Jonathan steepled his fingers, his voice low and reflective. "These aren't just random notes... They're pieces of a puzzle Gregor couldn't solve in time."

* * *

The mid-morning air carried a heavy unease as the trio ventured into town. Tumblebrook's usually lively streets were subdued, with small clusters of townspeople speaking in hushed tones. Whispers trailed Amelia, Clara, and Jonathan as they walked toward the library, the weight of the townspeople's scrutiny settling on their shoulders.

Outside the bakery, Edith Cranston stood speaking with Henry Swinton, the festival's most vocal vendor. Her sharp gaze flicked toward the group, her expression calculating.

Just as they passed, Dennis Griggs—a wiry man with deep-set eyes and a perpetual scowl—stepped out of the bakery, holding a paper bag. His piercing stare landed on Amelia, and he moved to block their path.

"You're stirring up trouble that doesn't need stirring," Dennis said, his voice low and biting. His words hung heavy in the air, drawing the attention of nearby townsfolk who feigned disinterest while leaning closer.

Amelia met his gaze steadily. "Trouble's already here, Dennis. I'm trying to stop it."

Dennis shifted, the crinkle of the bag in his hands audible as his grip tightened. "Some things are better left buried. Digging them up won't help anyone."

Clara stepped forward; her tone sharp. "And who decides that, Dennis? You? The council? Because from where I'm standing, the past isn't buried—it's bleeding into everything."

Dennis's jaw clenched. He leaned closer, lowering his voice so only the three could hear. "You think you're helping, poking around where you don't belong? You're not. You're putting yourselves in danger... and others, too."

Lady Grey, perched on Amelia's shoulder, let out a low, warning growl. Her ears flattened, her tail twitching with agitation. Dennis glanced at the cat, unease flickering briefly across his face before his usual scowl returned.

Amelia's voice was calm but unwavering. "If you've got something to say, Dennis, say it. Otherwise, move aside."

For a moment, Dennis hesitated, his eyes darting between them. Finally, he stepped back, his voice bitter. "Don't say I didn't warn you. Some things aren't worth knowing."

He turned and stalked away, leaving a tense silence in his wake. Clara watched him go; her hands clenched into fists. "That man knows more than he's letting on."

Jonathan nodded. "That wasn't just a warning. It was fear. He's afraid of what we'll find."

Amelia drew a steadying breath, her resolve hardening. "Then we're on the right track. Let's get to the library."

The library's heavy oak doors groaned as they swung open. Inside, the air was thick with the scent of aging paper and polished wood. The quiet was broken only by the faint hum of the heating system and the rustle of pages being turned by a lone reader in the corner. The atmosphere felt steeped in history—today, it seemed to hold secrets as well.

Clara took the lead, heading straight for the archival records. "I'll start in the archives," she said, motioning to the far corner. "Give me a few minutes."

Jonathan and Amelia found a table near a window, spreading Gregor's journal and Clara's notes across its surface. Lady Grey had followed them in, much to the librarian's disapproval. A quick reassurance from Amelia that the cat was well-behaved kept her at bay. Now, Lady Grey perched on the windowsill, her gaze flitting between Jonathan and the door to the archives.

"Do you think Gregor's markings were meant to lead someone here?" Amelia asked, her voice low.

Jonathan nodded, tracing a diagram in the journal with his finger. "It's possible. Libraries were often repositories of knowledge... and secrets. If Gregor believed something was hidden here, it's worth exploring."

Minutes later, Clara returned, her expression alight with discovery. She placed a large, leather-bound ledger on the table with a satisfying thud. "Found it," she said, flipping to a bookmarked page. "This ledger lists donations to the library from over two decades ago. Look at this entry: Elias Carradine, collection of sketches and correspondence."

Jonathan's eyes widened. "Carradine? The painter of *The Veil of Shadows*?"

Clara nodded. "It was a temporary exhibit. But there's no record of the collection being returned."

"It disappeared," Amelia murmured, realization dawning. "Just like the painting."

Jonathan's thoughts raced. "If Gregor knew about this, he might have been trying to recover the sketches to understand Carradine's intent. The painting and the mine—they're connected."

Clara tapped another entry in the ledger. "There's a note here—nearly illegible—but it mentions a key. It might have been used to access a special collection."

Jonathan glanced at Amelia, who rested a hand on her bag. "Do you think the key Gregor found...?"

"It has to be," she said.

Lady Grey let out a low growl, her tail twitching as she fixed her gaze on a distant door marked *Restricted Access.*

"What's behind there?" Amelia asked.

Clara shrugged. "Probably rare manuscripts or old records. It's locked."

Jonathan stood; determination clear in his expression. "Let's see if the key fits."

The lock was stiff, but after a bit of effort, the key turned with a satisfying click. The heavy door creaked open, revealing a dimly lit room lined with shelves. The cool air inside smelled strongly of aged paper and dust; the weight of history almost palpable.

Lady Grey darted in ahead of them, her movements deliberate. She paused near a shelf at the back, her tail flicking as she pawed at a low box.

Clara crouched down, pulling the box carefully from the shelf. The faded label read: *Carradine Collection.*

Amelia's breath hitched. "It's real."

Jonathan knelt beside Clara, gently lifting the lid. Inside were sketches, notes, and letters, each piece meticulously preserved. The sweeping lines and intricate details of the sketches were unmistakably Carradine's, echoing the fragment they had discovered in Gregor's journal. But it was the stack of letters that caught Jonathan's attention.

He unfolded one, scanning the elegant handwriting. His voice was steady as he read aloud, "'The mine holds more than ore. Its depths hide the truth of what we've done. To those who find this, know that shadows are not always cast by the light.'"

Clara's voice was barely above a whisper. "Carradine knew."

Amelia's pulse quickened. "Knew what?"

Jonathan shook his head, his eyes still on the letter. "We need more time to go through this, but one thing is clear: Carradine's work wasn't just art. It was a warning."

Lady Grey leapt gracefully onto the table, her eyes locking onto a specific sketch. Jonathan followed her gaze and pulled the piece forward. The drawing depicted a simple paintbox, but the brushstrokes surrounding it formed an abstract shape—one that Jonathan recognized immediately.

"The mine entrance," he murmured. "It's hidden within the brushwork."

Amelia leaned over his shoulder. "Do you think Gregor found something inside the paintbox?"

"Or something *about* the paintbox," Jonathan replied. "If Carradine's work held secrets, maybe Gregor uncovered one of them. And maybe that's why he was silenced."

Back at the inn, Jonathan spread the journal's pages across the dining table, the sketches and notes from the library laid out beside them. The faint light from the fireplace flickered over his face as he studied each piece, his analytical mind racing to connect the dots.

Amelia sat across from him, her chin resting on her hand. "Do you think we're chasing shadows?"

Jonathan glanced up, his expression thoughtful. "No. Shadows exist because of light. Gregor's journal, Carradine's letters, the marked locations—they all point to something tangible."

Clara entered the room carrying a folded newspaper clipping. "I found this while combing through the archives," she said, placing it on the table. The article detailed a heated town council meeting from years ago, where Gregor and Edith Cranston had clashed over the mine's future. The council had ultimately voted to block development, but the decision had been mired in controversy.

"Look at the names," Clara said, tapping the list of council members. "Edith Cranston, Henry Swinton, Dennis Griggs—all of them were on the council when the vote happened."

Jonathan's jaw tightened. "And now they're all warning us to stop digging."

Before Amelia could respond, her phone buzzed on the table. She picked it up, and her face froze. The message was short but chilling: *Stop, or you'll regret it.*

She turned the screen toward Jonathan and Clara. Her voice was steady, but her eyes betrayed her unease. "It seems someone doesn't appreciate our investigation."

Jonathan's expression hardened. "We're getting close. Close enough to scare someone."

Lady Grey jumped onto the table, her tail swishing as she sniffed the journal. Her intense gaze seemed to echo Jonathan's thoughts: the shadows in Tumblebrook were growing darker, but they were closing in on the truth.

The inn had grown quiet as night deepened. Jonathan stayed up late, poring over the journal and cross-referencing it with Clara's notes. Each location Gregor marked seemed to correspond to a significant event in Tumblebrook's history—a fire at the coppersmith's shop, a collapse near the library, and the mine disaster that had sparked decades of speculation.

Lady Grey stretched out beside him, her paws twitching as if chasing something in her dreams. Jonathan absentmindedly scratched behind her ears, muttering to himself, "Every event was a diversion. A way to hide something bigger."

He flipped back to the sketch of the paintbox, his eyes narrowing. The brushstrokes framing it now seemed deliberate—forming an abstract map of the mine's entrance, cleverly disguised within the drawing. Gregor had been leaving breadcrumbs, trusting someone would follow them.

Lady Grey yawned and sat up; her ears pricked toward the door. Moments later, a soft knock echoed through the quiet inn.

Jonathan stood, his pulse quickening. Who would visit at this hour?

Amelia appeared at the top of the stairs; her expression wary. "Who is it?"

Jonathan opened the door cautiously, revealing a figure cloaked in shadows. As they stepped forward into the dim light of the hallway, their face became clear: Edith Cranston.

Her voice trembled as she spoke. "We need to talk," she said, glancing nervously over her shoulder. "Before it's too late."

Chapter 7

Tangled Threads

The early morning light filtered through the lace curtains of The Lakeside Inn, but Amelia Farnsworth barely noticed. She stood in the parlor, arms crossed, staring at the array of documents strewn across the coffee table. Clara and Dr. Westwood sat nearby, their expressions equally focused. Lady Grey observed them from her perch on the windowsill, her amber eyes sharp and attentive. The unexpected visit from Edith and her cryptic request the previous night hung heavy over the room. But there was more they needed to understand before they could entertain any conversation with Edith.

"An apprentice," Amelia said finally, her voice cutting through the heavy silence. "Carradine had an apprentice. Someone who worked alongside him, who might understand what his paintings were meant to reveal."

Clara adjusted her glasses and nodded; her pen poised over her notebook. "It's in the notes we found yesterday. He references 'E' as helping with *The Veil of Shadows*. But there's no full name, just initials."

Dr. Westwood leaned back, tapping his chin thoughtfully. "An apprentice would have been privy to Carradine's creative process—maybe even his secrets. If this 'E' is still alive, they might have the missing piece to all of this."

Amelia flipped to a fresh page in her notebook. "Then we need to find them. If Gregor knew about the apprentice, it could explain why he was targeted."

"I'll start by checking the local art community archives," Clara said, already jotting down a list. "Carradine's apprentice would've left some trace, even if they kept a low profile."

Amelia nodded. "I'll call some of the older members of the Artists' Collective. They might remember someone who worked closely with Carradine."

Lady Grey meowed softly, breaking the tension, and Amelia couldn't help but smile. "Don't worry, Lady. You'll get credit for solving this mystery, too."

The day unfolded with a series of interruptions that made focusing on the investigation nearly impossible. A large group of unexpected guests arrived at the inn, rerouted from another lodge due to a plumbing issue. The Lakeside Inn, usually a sanctuary of calm, turned into a whirlwind of activity.

The chaos began with the arrival of an oversized tour bus that struggled to fit into the inn's modest parking lot. Amelia greeted the guests with her usual warmth, masking the anxiety bubbling beneath the surface. Each guest seemed to have a unique request: extra towels, specific dietary needs, and, in one case, a demand for a room with a "perfect view" of the lake—something Amelia couldn't guarantee with the inn already full.

Inside, Clara tried to maintain order in the dining area, which had become a hive of commotion. Two children darted between tables, narrowly avoiding a server carrying a tray of hot tea. Their mother scrolled through her phone, oblivious, while a retired schoolteacher chastised the children for their unruly behavior.

Dr. Westwood retreated to the study, his usual calm visibly fraying. He'd been mapping out Gregor's notes when a guest barged in to complain about the lack of fresh pillows. He redirected them to the front desk with a tight-lipped smile, his concentration shattered.

In the kitchen, Greta, the part-time cook, muttered under her breath as she scrambled to prepare additional meals for the unexpected guests. The clatter of pots and pans echoed through the inn, a discordant backdrop to the morning's mayhem.

Lady Grey, unfazed by the chaos, perched on the reception desk like a serene overseer. Occasionally, she swiped at a pen or watched the guests with curiosity, her calm demeanor a stark contrast to the frenetic energy around her.

By mid-afternoon, tensions reached a peak when a vase went missing from the parlor, and a guest accused a housekeeper of stealing their wallet. Amelia found herself mediating between the two, trying to diffuse the situation while suppressing her growing frustration.

During a rare quiet moment, Clara pulled Amelia aside. "Something feels off," she said in a low voice. "All this chaos... it's too convenient, given how close we're getting."

Amelia frowned. "You think someone's trying to throw us off?"

Clara's eyes scanned the bustling dining room, landing on a man sitting alone in the corner. His scruffy appearance and weathered coat were unremarkable, but his furtive glances told another story. His eyes lingered on Amelia and Clara just a moment too long before returning to his coffee.

"Keep an eye on him," Amelia said, her voice barely above a whisper. "I'll handle the guests, but we need to stay sharp."

Clara's jaw tightened. "Whoever's behind this might be closer than we think."

That evening, after the commotion had finally subsided, Clara set up her laptop at the kitchen table to analyze the town's financial records. Her recent discovery of irregularities in the town council's funds had piqued her curiosity, and she was determined to uncover more.

Clara's workspace was a controlled chaos of papers, notebooks, and her laptop. The glow of the screen illuminated her determined expression as she scrolled through spreadsheets and transaction records. A steaming mug of tea sat forgotten beside her.

"There's definitely something fishy here," Clara said, her voice tinged with excitement. "Look at this. Henry Swinton received a significant payment six months ago—'consulting fees' from a company tied to the old mining operation."

She clicked on another tab, pointing to another entry. "And here's another transfer, this one to Edith Cranston. It's labeled as an 'art commission,' but the amount is suspiciously high."

Amelia leaned over her shoulder. "That's a lot of money for consulting and art. What are they really being paid for?"

Clara smirked. "That's the million-dollar question—or, in this case, the thousand-dollar one."

She cross-referenced the transactions. "The timing is too coincidental. The payments coincide with key dates: the redevelopment proposal, the council's vote to block it, and..." She scrolled further. "Six months ago, when Gregor stopped receiving payments."

Lady Grey leapt onto the table, her tail flicking against Clara's arm. The cat's sudden focus on the screen felt intentional, drawing a smile from Clara. "Even she knows we're onto something."

Clara clicked on another record. "North Star Holdings. They're still active, even though the mine's been abandoned for years."

Amelia's expression darkened. "If Swinton and Cranston were involved, they're protecting something. Something worth hiding."

Jonathan entered the kitchen, shaking off the evening chill. "What did I miss?"

Clara turned her laptop toward him. "North Star Holdings is funneling money to council members, including Edith Cranston. And they've been doing it for years."

Jonathan frowned, studying the records. "They were pushing the mine's redevelopment. If they're still active, it means there's more at stake than we thought."

Amelia's thoughts raced. "They must be protecting what's in the mine. Gregor's journal said the mine held more than ore. What if it's true value is something North Star Holdings can't risk exposing?"

Lady Grey growled softly; her eyes fixed on a paper that had fallen to the floor. Clara picked it up. It was a deed for the land surrounding the mine entrance. The name on the deed was nearly illegible, but the signature at the bottom stood out: *E.C.*

Amelia's eyes narrowed. "E.C.... Edith Cranston. She's more involved than she's letting on."

Jonathan's voice was calm but firm. "If Edith knows about the apprentice, she might know exactly what's hidden in the mine."

Clara hesitated. "Do we dig deeper into her records?"

Amelia shook her head. "Not yet. If she suspects we're looking into her finances, she'll cover her tracks."

Jonathan crossed his arms. "Then what's our next move?"

Amelia's gaze hardened. "We confront her. But carefully. Edith Cranston isn't someone to underestimate."

Lady Grey jumped onto the table, her tail swishing as if to say, *Finally.*

Chapter 8

Clarity and Cunning

Rain lashed against the windows of The Lakeside Inn, an insistent rhythm that matched Clara's restless thoughts. She sat in the study, surrounded by papers, notebooks, and her ever-reliable laptop. The faint glow of the screen illuminated her furrowed brow as she pieced together the tangled web of discoveries from the past few days.

Lady Grey perched on a nearby chair, her amber eyes focused intently on the desk as though she, too, were invested in unraveling the mystery. The cat's calm presence was oddly reassuring, a counterpoint to the storm both outside and within.

"All right, Lady," Clara murmured, scrolling through her spreadsheets. "Let's make sense of this mess."

The financial records had revealed a convoluted trail of payments, all leading back to North Star Holdings. But the true revelation came earlier that day—a deed linking Edith Cranston to the land surrounding the abandoned mine. Combined with Gregor Steele's journal, Edith was emerging as a central figure in a decades-old conspiracy.

Clara scribbled Edith's name onto her notepad, underlining it twice. "She's in the thick of it," she muttered. "But why hide the connection to the mine? And what's the apprentice's role in all this?"

Lady Grey let out a soft trill and leapt onto the desk, nudging a folded piece of paper buried beneath a stack of notes. Clara picked it up, frowning. It was an old letter, the ink faded but legible, bearing the Tumblebrook Historical Society's crest.

"What's this?" Clara unfolded the letter carefully. Addressed to Elias Carradine, it referenced an excavation near the mine. Her breath caught as she read the final line: *The chambers beneath the council hall must remain sealed. Some truths are better left buried.*

Her pulse quickened. "Chambers beneath the council hall...?"

Amelia entered moments later, drawn by the urgency in Clara's voice. Together, they studied the letter, its implications chilling. The study, usually a tranquil haven, buzzed with tension. Outside, the storm added to the atmosphere, its muffled roar a constant backdrop. Amelia closed the door to block the distant clatter of guest activity, but the sense of unease lingered.

"If there are hidden chambers under the council hall, it could explain why Edith and the others are so desperate to keep everything quiet," Amelia said, her brow furrowed. "But why would Carradine have been involved?"

"Maybe the chambers hold something he painted about in *The Veil of Shadows,*" Clara suggested. "Or something that inspired it."

Before Amelia could respond, a sharp knock on the study door interrupted them. She sighed and opened it to reveal Beth, a flustered housekeeper juggling an armful of linens.

"Ms. Farnsworth, one of the guests says their radiator isn't working. Should I call the repairman?"

Amelia shook her head. "No, I'll handle it. Thanks, Beth. Just leave those here."

As Beth left, Amelia turned back to Clara, her expression apologetic. "It's been one thing after another today."

Clara waved it off, already engrossed in the letter again. "Multitasking is our specialty."

Lady Grey, sensing the renewed focus, pawed at the letter, as if urging them forward.

Moments later, another interruption—a loud crash from the kitchen. Amelia stiffened, muttering under her breath as she left the room to investigate. When she returned, exasperation was written across her face.

"Broken mugs," she said, sinking into a chair. "At least the guests are finally settling down."

Clara raised an eyebrow. "You think all these distractions are just coincidence?"

Amelia hesitated, then shook her head. "No. It's too much. This chaos started as soon as we began making real progress. Someone's trying to slow us down."

Lady Grey meowed softly, her tail twitching as she jumped to the windowsill, staring into the rain-soaked night. Clara tapped her pen against the table, her mind racing. "Then we'd better work faster. Whoever's behind this is running out of time."

Lady Grey's abrupt leap from the windowsill and swift exit from the room signaled something new. Clara and Amelia exchanged a glance before following the cat into the hall. Curiosity and unease hung heavy in the air. If distractions were mounting, it meant their next step could bring them closer to the truth—or danger.

* * *

The rain had eased by the time they reached the council hall. Its imposing stone facade loomed over the empty square, illuminated by the dim glow of streetlamps. Lady Grey darted ahead, slipping into the shadows as Amelia and Clara approached the heavy wooden doors.

"We're breaking into the council hall in the middle of the night," Clara whispered, half-amused, half-nervous. "This feels... dramatic."

Amelia smirked. "Think of it as after-hours research."

The door creaked open, and they slipped inside. The grand

corridors, lined with faded carpets and portraits of long-gone council members, were eerily silent. Guided by the letter, they made their way to the basement, flashlights cutting through the darkness.

Lady Grey led them unerringly to a door marked *Storage*. Amelia tried the handle, and to their surprise, it turned easily. Inside, the room was cluttered with forgotten artifacts, old furniture, and dusty filing cabinets.

"Over here," Amelia said, kneeling near a section of newer tiles on the floor. She traced the edges with her fingers. "There's a seam."

Clara crouched beside her, pulling a multitool from her pocket. With careful effort, they pried up the tiles, revealing a hidden hatch. Lady Grey hopped onto its edge, peering into the darkness below.

"You've got to be kidding me," Clara whispered. "There's actually a hidden chamber."

Amelia shone her flashlight into the opening, illuminating a narrow staircase descending into the shadows. "Ready?"

Clara hesitated, then sighed. "I didn't sign up for spelunking, but let's do this."

The air grew damp and cold as they descended, their flashlights casting long shadows across rough stone walls. The chamber was larger than they'd expected, its shelves lined with crates and papers coated in years of dust. At the center stood a pedestal, its surface scattered with yellowed documents.

Clara approached cautiously, her flashlight illuminating the papers. She picked one up, her breath catching at the title: *Blueprints for the Mine Expansion—Tumblebrook Council, 1923.*

"These plans show tunnels that extend far beyond what's on any official map," she said, her voice tight with awe.

Amelia joined her, scanning the blueprints. "This must be what Gregor was trying to uncover. These tunnels lead somewhere important."

A noise behind them made both women freeze. They turned, flashlights landing on a figure standing at the top of the stairs. Edith

Cranston descended slowly, holding a lantern. Her expression, usually composed, was edged with cold fury.

"You shouldn't be here," Edith said, her voice calm but steely. "You don't understand what you're meddling with."

Before they could respond, Henry Swinton appeared behind her, holding a padlock and chain. His jovial air was gone, replaced by something darker.

"They've seen too much," Henry said simply, handing the chain to Edith. She moved to secure the hatch, her hands steady despite the tension crackling in the room.

Clara's voice was sharp. "You're going to lock us in here? What is wrong with you?"

Edith met her gaze, unflinching. "You're meddling in things you don't understand. The truth you're chasing? It'll destroy this town."

As the hatch slammed shut, Clara and Amelia were plunged into darkness. Lady Grey let out a sharp yowl, pawing at the sealed entrance.

"We'll find a way out," Amelia said firmly, her voice steady despite the fear in her eyes. "We always do."

Lady Grey meowed again, drawing their attention to a discolored section of the wall. Clara pressed her hand against it, feeling a faint draft. "There's another way out."

Amelia nodded, determination hardening her features. "Let's find it."

With Lady Grey leading the way, they pushed into the narrow passage, their resolve stronger than ever. Whatever secrets lay at the heart of Tumblebrook, they were closer than ever to unearthing them.

Chapter 9

Hidden Reveals

Amelia Farnsworth's breath came in short gasps as she crawled through the narrow passage. The stone walls pressed close on either side, and the faint draft carried the scent of damp earth. Behind her, Clara's flashlight beam jittered as her friend maneuvered through the dark space, muttering occasional protests about the claustrophobic conditions. Lady Grey darted ahead, her sleek form moving with an agility that seemed effortless, even in the confined space.

"Remind me," Clara grumbled, her voice echoing faintly, "why do we keep trusting this cat's instincts?"

Amelia managed a smile despite their predicament. "Because she's never wrong."

Ahead, Lady Grey paused, her amber eyes glowing in the darkness. She let out a soft meow and waited, her tail flicking impatiently. Amelia quickened her pace, reaching a slight widening in the tunnel that revealed a small grate. Pressing her ear to the metal, she strained to hear faint voices filtering through—too muffled to discern but unmistakably human.

"There's someone up there," Amelia whispered.

Clara edged closer. "Whoever it is, let's hope they're not as eager to lock us in again."

The grate was loose, and with a sharp tug, Amelia managed to dislodge it. The metal clattered softly onto the stone floor, and she pushed the barrier aside to reveal a narrow staircase. Cautiously, the two women ascended, their steps muffled on the worn stone.

The staircase led to an old utility room filled with forgotten tools and a thick layer of dust. Amelia eased open the door and peered into the hallway beyond. It was quiet, though the faint hum of fluorescent lights suggested they were still within the town hall.

"We're out," Clara said with a relieved sigh. She brushed off her knees and shot a look at Lady Grey, who was grooming herself with an air of indifference. "Now what?"

The escape hadn't been seamless. As they navigated the dimly lit halls, every creak of the floorboards set their nerves on edge. Clara gripped her flashlight tightly, her knuckles white, while Amelia glanced over her shoulder, half-expecting Edith or Henry to appear.

"This place gives me the creeps," Clara muttered. "How did we not know about these passages?"

"I doubt many people do," Amelia replied. "That's probably why Edith and Henry felt safe using them."

Lady Grey darted ahead, pausing suddenly with her ears pricked forward. Amelia followed the cat's gaze and froze. At the end of the corridor, a faint sliver of light seeped through a crack in the wall.

"Looks like another way out," Amelia whispered.

They moved toward the light, discovering an old wooden door. Amelia pressed her ear to it, listening carefully. When she heard nothing, she turned the handle, and the door creaked open to reveal a small storage room crowded with cleaning supplies. A flickering bulb overhead cast erratic shadows.

"We're still in the building," Clara noted, scanning the room. "But at least we're out of that creepy basement."

Amelia spotted a small window on the far wall. She pushed it open, letting in a rush of cool night air. "This is our way out."

Clara hesitated, eyeing her dusty clothes. "I'm starting to think helping you run an inn didn't prepare me for this kind of adventure."

"You're doing great," Amelia said with a wry smile. "Now, come on."

With effort, they climbed through the window and landed in a patch of overgrown grass. Lady Grey followed with a graceful leap, landing silently beside them. The night air was crisp, carrying the faint scent of rain and earth.

Amelia brushed off her hands and surveyed their surroundings. "Let's get back to the inn and regroup. We're not done yet."

Back at The Lakeside Inn, the two women spread their notes and documents across the dining table. Lady Grey perched on a chair, her sharp eyes following their every movement. Amelia grabbed a notebook and began sketching out a timeline, starting with Gregor's discovery of the blueprints and ending with their escape.

"Okay," Amelia said, circling the date of Gregor's death. "This is the catalyst. Whatever he found—or threatened to reveal—triggered everything that's happened since."

Clara nodded, drawing a line from Gregor's death to the series of festival incidents. "The fight between Gregor and Edith at that council meeting happened two weeks earlier. From his journal, we know he'd been questioning their decisions long before that."

"And Edith wouldn't act alone," Amelia said. "Henry's involvement is clear now, but he's not the mastermind. Someone else is pulling the strings."

Clara tapped her pen against the notepad. "What about the festival sabotage? Missing art supplies, vandalized booths... they feel like distractions. Maybe there's a pattern we've missed."

Amelia leaned back; her gaze fixed on the timeline. "It's like they're trying to keep the town focused on surface-level chaos while something bigger happens behind the scenes."

"And Gregor saw through it," Clara added. "That's why they silenced him."

As the hours ticked by, they began eliminating false leads. The missing art supplies, it turned out, had been misplaced by an over-worked volunteer. The vandalized booths, initially suspected to be deliberate sabotage, were the result of unsupervised teenagers.

"It's like clearing brush," Clara said, crossing out another dead end. "The more we eliminate, the clearer the real picture gets."

Lady Grey suddenly leapt onto the table, nudging a sheet of paper with her paw. Amelia picked it up, recognizing it immediately as an entry from Gregor's journal. "'The festival rehearsals are more than they seem,'" she read aloud. "'Hidden in plain sight.'"

Clara's eyes widened. "The rehearsals! Remember the noise during the council meetings? We dismissed it as performers practicing."

Amelia's pulse quickened. "What if the rehearsals were a cover? Someone could have been eavesdropping—or worse, using them to hide something."

Determined to investigate, they headed to the festival grounds, where a late-night rehearsal was underway. Music drifted through the air as performers milled about the stage, their voices mingling in a chaotic but cheerful symphony.

Amelia scanned the area, her gaze landing on a shadowy figure near the rehearsal tent. "Clara," she whispered. "Do you see that?"

Clara followed her gaze. "That's not a performer."

They approached cautiously, weaving through props and folding chairs until they were close enough to see the figure clearly. It was a man, his face partially obscured by a hat and scarf. He held a small recording device, his focus entirely on the stage.

"Excuse me," Amelia said sharply.

The man flinched, stuffing the device into his pocket and turning to leave. Clara moved quickly, blocking his path.

"Not so fast," she said. "Who are you, and what are you doing here?"

The man hesitated before sighing. He removed his hat, revealing a face both familiar and unexpected.

"Dennis Griggs," Amelia said, her voice heavy with suspicion. "Why am I not surprised?"

Dennis shrugged; his expression guarded. "You're barking up the wrong tree. I'm just here to... check on things."

"With a recording device?" Clara challenged. "That's not exactly casual behavior."

Dennis's jaw tightened. "You wouldn't understand."

"Try us," Amelia said, folding her arms.

Dennis's shoulders slumped as he realized there was no easy escape. He glanced over his shoulder, as if expecting someone to emerge from the shadows and intervene. When no one did, he sighed and muttered, "Fine. You're right. I've been keeping tabs on Edith and Henry. They've been planning something, and I'm trying to figure out what it is before it's too late."

Clara's eyes narrowed as she studied him. "You expect us to believe you're working against them? You've been lurking around for weeks, Dennis. You've never exactly been transparent."

Dennis raised his hands defensively. "I know how it looks, okay? But I'm not on their side. I've seen what they're capable of. Edith's been using the festival to cover her tracks. She's hiding something big, and it's tied to that mine."

Amelia exchanged a glance with Clara, her instincts torn. On the one hand, Dennis's story fit the pieces they'd already uncovered. On the other, his motives and trustworthiness remained murky.

"If you're serious about stopping her," Amelia said, her voice firm but measured, "you need to tell us everything you know. No more half-truths. No more secrets."

Dennis hesitated, his jaw tightening as he weighed his options. Finally, he reached into his coat pocket and pulled out the recording device. "This is everything I've got. Conversations I've overheard, meetings they thought were private. Edith's been orchestrating the entire thing—from Gregor's silence to the festival disruptions."

Clara took the device, her expression skeptical. "And you just happened to be in the right places at the right times? Why?"

Dennis looked away, his voice quieter now. "Because I knew what they were doing wasn't right. At first, I thought it was just about money—the usual backroom deals. But when Gregor started asking questions... it got darker."

"Darker how?" Amelia pressed.

"They're protecting something in that mine," Dennis said, his eyes locking with Amelia's. "And it's worth more than we can imagine. Edith's willing to do whatever it takes to keep it hidden—even if it means hurting more people."

The weight of his words hung in the air, heavy and foreboding. Lady Grey, who had been quietly observing, let out a soft growl, her tail flicking in irritation. Amelia reached down to stroke her fur, drawing comfort from the cat's steady presence.

"If what you're saying is true," Amelia said, "then we're running out of time."

Dennis nodded grimly. "We are. And if you're smart, you'll stay out of it. Edith doesn't play fair."

"Neither do we," Clara said, her voice firm. "Now, let's hear what's on this recording."

Chapter 10

The Final Palette

D r. Jonathan Westwood adjusted the cuffs of his crisp shirt, his movements precise as he surveyed the Lakeside Inn's grand parlor. Sunlight filtered through lace curtains, casting a golden glow over the assembled guests, but the light did little to dispel the tension in the room. The faint creak of chairs and murmurs of unease underscored the charged atmosphere. Chairs had been arranged in a wide circle, positioning Edith Cranston, Henry Swinton, Dennis Griggs, and several others like reluctant actors awaiting their cue.

Amelia Farnsworth stood near the fireplace, arms crossed, her gaze steady as it swept over the group. The weight of Gregor Steele's death and the discoveries that had followed pressed heavily on her, but she refused to let it show. Clara perched at the corner of a side table, notebook in hand, her pen poised. Lady Grey, ever the picture of poise, occupied the best seat in the room—a plush armchair— curled up as though orchestrating the entire gathering.

"Thank you all for joining us," Dr. Westwood began, his voice calm yet commanding. He stepped into the center of the room, hands clasped behind his back, the very image of a seasoned investigator. "I imagine you're wondering why you've been summoned here. The truth is, the events of the past few weeks—Gregor Steele's murder, the sabotage at the festival, and the secrets surrounding the mine—are all connected. Today, we intend to reveal those connections."

A ripple of murmurs broke out. Edith Cranston's sharp eyes narrowed, betraying nothing. Henry Swinton shifted uncomfortably, gripping the arms of his chair as though bracing for impact. Dennis Griggs kept his gaze fixed on the floor, his face tight with unease. The remaining attendees—council members and local artisans—exchanged nervous glances.

"Let's begin," Dr. Westwood continued, cutting through the whispers. "This all began with Gregor Steele. He wasn't just a skilled coppersmith; he was a man who cared deeply for this community. His death, however, was no accident."

Amelia stepped forward, her voice steady despite the tightness in her chest. "Gregor's journals led us to the mine, to the hidden chambers beneath the council hall, and to the shadowy dealings of North Star Holdings. His discoveries uncovered truths that some of you would have preferred stayed buried."

Edith's lips thinned, but she held her silence. Henry's eyes darted toward her, his unease impossible to hide.

"The mine," Dr. Westwood said, picking up the thread, "was not merely a failed venture. Decades ago, the council discovered something hidden deep within its tunnels—artifacts of significant artistic and historical value. Elias Carradine, the artist behind *The Veil of Shadows*, knew of these relics. His paintings contained clues to their location."

Clara flipped open a journal, holding it aloft. "Carradine's apprentice, known only as 'E.C.,' worked closely with him to embed those clues into his art. That apprentice, we've now uncovered, was none other than Edith Cranston."

A collective gasp rippled through the room. Edith's stone-cold expression faltered, the slightest twitch of her jaw betraying her discomfort.

"Elias Carradine trusted you," Dr. Westwood said, his tone sharp. "You knew about the artifacts and the mine's secrets. But instead of safeguarding his legacy, you turned to greed. After Carradine's death, you kept the knowledge to yourself, waiting for the right moment to claim what you believed was yours."

Edith's voice, when she finally spoke, was low and steely. "You speak as though you know everything. But you don't. Not even close."

"Then enlighten us," Amelia challenged.

The room fell silent. Edith stood slowly, her movements deliberate as she turned to face the group.

"Carradine was no fool," she said, her voice tinged with bitterness. "The artifacts hidden in the mine—smuggled treasures from Europe during the war—were meant to stay hidden. He believed they were too dangerous to surface, so he buried their secrets in his art. He trusted me to keep them safe. But this town..." Her hand gestured broadly. "This town is built on greed. When the council caught wind of what was in the mine, they wanted to exploit it. I stopped them once. Gregor... he threatened to undo everything."

She faltered, her voice cracking.

"Gregor discovered your connection to Carradine," Dr. Westwood said, his tone gentler now. "He found the blueprints hidden in the council hall. He threatened to expose the truth."

Edith's eyes flashed with anger. "I didn't kill Gregor!"

Henry Swinton's chair creaked as he shifted. His face was pale, his eyes avoiding Edith's. The room grew still as Dr. Westwood turned his attention to him.

"You didn't act alone, did you, Henry?" he asked, his voice laced with quiet authority. "The payments from North Star Holdings went to you. In exchange, you kept the council's secrets."

Henry's voice cracked when he spoke. "I didn't mean for it to go this far. The council promised us all a cut when the mine reopened. But Gregor... he wouldn't stop digging. He threatened everything. Edith said we could warn him—scare him into silence."

Edith turned on him sharply. "Don't you dare pin this on me! I told you to warn him, not kill him!"

Henry's voice rose, raw with desperation. "He wouldn't stop! I didn't mean to push him that hard. It was an accident!"

A heavy silence fell over the room, Henry's confession hanging in the air. Edith slumped into her chair, her face pale and hollow.

Dr. Westwood's steady voice broke the stillness. "Gregor Steele's death was no accident, Mr. Swinton. You made a choice, and you will face justice for it. Edith, for all your talk of protecting Carradine's legacy, you hid the truth for your own gain."

Amelia folded her arms, her voice calm but resolute. "Carradine trusted you, Edith. You betrayed him. Those artifacts were meant to be protected, not exploited."

The next day, clear skies and crisp autumn air ushered Tumblebrook into a new chapter. Henry Swinton was taken into custody, his role in the conspiracy now public knowledge. The artifacts Carradine had so desperately hidden were transferred to the Tumblebrook Historical Society for preservation. Edith Cranston, though not charged, faced the court of public opinion, her reputation irreparably tarnished.

The fall festival resumed with renewed vigor. The square buzzed with life—laughter, music, and the scent of roasted chestnuts filling the air. For the first time in weeks, Tumblebrook felt free from the shadows of its past.

At The Lakeside Inn, Amelia, Clara, and Dr. Westwood sat on the porch, steaming mugs of cider in hand. Lady Grey lounged contentedly at their feet, her tail flicking lazily.

"Well," Clara said, watching the festivalgoers with a smile, "that's one way to kick off fall."

"Tumblebrook does have a knack for excitement," Amelia replied. "Let's hope next year is quieter."

Dr. Westwood chuckled. "Something tells me mysteries will always find you, Amelia."

Amelia shook her head, though her smile hinted at agreement. "I couldn't solve them without all of you... and Lady Grey, of course."

At her name, Lady Grey stretched languidly, as if claiming credit for the entire case. The group laughed, their bond strengthened by the trials they'd faced.

As the festival carried on and peace settled over Tumblebrook, Amelia allowed herself a deep breath. Whatever mystery came next, she knew she—and her team—would be ready.

Chapter 11

Harmony and Hints

The morning dawned with a golden glow over Tumblebrook. The Lakeside Inn stood proud, bathed in sunlight as mist lifted gently from the lake. It was the kind of serene morning that made Amelia Farnsworth pause, breathe, and savor the simple joys of small-town life. The weight of the past few weeks—the revelations, the tension of the investigation—felt lighter now, as though the town itself had taken a deep, collective breath.

From the inn's porch, Amelia sipped her steaming coffee, letting the rich aroma ground her. Her gaze drifted over the town square, where children laughed as they chased each other, and couples strolled hand-in-hand, ready to resume their festival activities. A slow smile touched her lips as she noticed Clara chatting animatedly with a volunteer from the historical society near the bookstore. Even those who had been wary of the investigation now seemed at ease.

Lady Grey perched on the railing beside her, amber eyes squinting in the sunlight, the picture of feline contentment. She let out a quiet trill, a reminder of her presence.

"I know, Lady," Amelia murmured with a chuckle, scratching

behind the cat's ears. "We couldn't have done it without you. You've earned your rest, haven't you?"

The cat blinked slowly, an acknowledgment of her importance in solving the mystery that had rattled their peaceful town.

Behind her, the front door creaked open, and Dr. Westwood stepped onto the porch. He carried his own cup of coffee, his demeanor as calm and polished as ever.

"Good morning, Amelia," he said with a nod, his sharp eyes scanning the square. "It seems Tumblebrook is beginning to settle back into itself. Peaceful, isn't it?"

"It is," Amelia agreed. "You'd hardly think we were in the middle of a whirlwind investigation just days ago. It's amazing how quickly life returns to normal."

Dr. Westwood smiled faintly. "Normal is relative. For a town like this, normal seems to involve its fair share of intrigue."

Amelia laughed softly, shaking her head. "Fair enough. But I'll take the calm while it lasts."

He settled into a chair beside her, setting his coffee on the small table between them. "The resolution of the mine artifacts and Edith's confession... you handled it admirably, Amelia. I'd say the town owes you a debt of gratitude."

"Not just me," she replied modestly. "Clara, Lady Grey, and you all played your parts. We're a good team, wouldn't you say?"

Dr. Westwood nodded, his smile deepening. "A formidable one."

By late morning, Amelia wandered through town, soaking in the vibrant energy of a community restored. Townsfolk stopped her to chat, many offering heartfelt thanks—a relieved baker pressing a warm loaf of bread into her hands, a group of children recounting how Lady Grey had "solved the mystery."

"You're a hero, Ms. Farnsworth!" one of the younger boys declared with wide-eyed sincerity.

"Lady Grey's the real hero," Amelia replied with a grin, earning a round of giggles.

The square buzzed with activity as volunteers from the historical society carefully loaded documents and artifacts into a waiting truck, bound for safekeeping at the museum. On the steps of the council hall, a group of older residents debated what the mine's treasures would mean for Tumblebrook's legacy.

Amelia's steps carried her to Clara's bookstore, where her friend stood outside, rearranging a display of books featuring local history and legends. A fresh chalkboard sign read: *Mystery and Lore of Tumblebrook – Special Discount!* Clara spotted Amelia and waved her over.

"Morning, Amelia," Clara greeted, brushing her hands on her apron. "How's life at the inn? Still peaceful?"

"Surprisingly so," Amelia said. "Feels strange, doesn't it? Like the quiet after a storm."

Clara nodded thoughtfully. "We needed it. Everyone's been walking on eggshells since Gregor's death. Now, people can focus on rebuilding trust—and maybe appreciating the history they almost lost."

Amelia ran her fingers along the spines of the displayed books. "Do you think people will want to hear the full story? About the artifacts?"

"Give it time," Clara said. "For now, they'll just be glad to have their festival back. The rest will settle into legend, like it always does."

Lady Grey leapt onto the display table, drawing a soft laugh from Clara. "She's quite the celebrity now, isn't she? Maybe I should feature her in the window."

"She'd love it," Amelia replied dryly. "As long as she gets her fair share of treats."

The day passed in a gentle rhythm. Guests at the inn came and went, and Amelia returned to her routines with quiet satisfaction. By evening, she was setting up for dinner service in the dining room. Clara had volunteered to cook, and the rich aroma of her beef stew filled the air, mingling with the faint scent of woodsmoke from the fireplace.

As Amelia arranged the last table, the bell above the front door jingled. She turned to find a man standing in the entryway, a leather satchel slung over his shoulder. He was tall and sharply dressed in a tailored coat, his dark hair flecked with silver at the temples. His quiet, deliberate presence reminded her of Dr. Westwood.

"Good evening," Amelia greeted with a welcoming smile. "Welcome to the Lakeside Inn. Are you checking in?"

The man nodded, his smile polite but reserved. "Yes, ma'am. I believe I have a reservation. Thomas Marlowe."

Amelia checked the ledger. "Yes, here you are. Room three. Visiting for business or pleasure, Mr. Marlowe?"

"A bit of both," he replied cryptically, his tone smooth but noncommittal. "I've heard Tumblebrook is full of history. Thought I'd see for myself."

Amelia paused, studying him. His sharp gaze roved over the inn's polished wood and old portraits. It wasn't the casual curiosity of a tourist; it was something more deliberate.

Before she could ask further, Lady Grey trotted in and stopped abruptly, staring at the newcomer. Her tail twitched, and she let out a low, inquisitive meow.

Marlowe's smile softened as he looked down. "Ah, the famous Lady Grey. I've heard about you."

Amelia raised an eyebrow. "Heard about her?"

"Small towns have their stories," Marlowe said with a shrug. "I'm sure I'll hear plenty more during my stay."

"I'm sure you will," Amelia replied, curiosity sparking.

As Marlowe headed upstairs, his deliberate movements left Amelia with the distinct impression his arrival was no coincidence. Lady Grey remained rooted, staring after him, her ears twitching.

"What are you thinking, Lady?" Amelia murmured, scratching the cat's ears. Lady Grey meowed softly, her tail flicking in that enigmatic way of hers.

"Who was that?" Clara asked, appearing with a tray of dishes.

"A guest," Amelia said. "Thomas Marlowe. Seems harmless enough, but there's something about him..."

"Suspicious already?" Clara teased.

Amelia's smile was faint. "Let's just say he's very interested in Tumblebrook's history—and he knew Lady Grey by name."

Clara's curiosity flickered. "Maybe he's just a history buff. Or maybe you've got your next mystery."

Amelia glanced toward Lady Grey, now lounging by the fireplace, her ears still alert. The Lakeside Inn was calm again—for now. But Amelia couldn't shake the feeling another mystery was waiting just around the corner.

Chapter 12

Shadows from the Past

The day following Thomas Marlowe's arrival at the Lakeside Inn was deceptively calm. Sunlight streamed through the wide parlor windows, bathing everything in a golden warmth as if nature itself sought to reassure the town that all was well. Yet Amelia Farnsworth couldn't shake a sense of unease—a whisper of something unresolved lingering just at the edge of her mind.

Standing by the window with a fresh cup of tea in hand, she gazed out at the lake. Gentle ripples spread across its surface like echoes of the past. For a moment, the events of recent weeks replayed in her mind—Gregor's murder, the mine's secrets, and the artifacts Elias Carradine had fought so hard to protect. Tumblebrook was a town of quiet complexities, its surface charm concealing stories deeper than most realized. Her grip on the teacup tightened as her thoughts turned to Thomas Marlowe. His deliberate interest in the town—and his strange familiarity with Lady Grey—felt far too coincidental.

The fall festival continued, and the townspeople were eager to leave behind the chaos that had overshadowed it. Vendors sold their wares with renewed energy, children prepared to return to school, and routines were reestablishing themselves. Familiar faces at the inn smiled again, relieved the shadow of Gregor Steele's death had lifted.

Still, Amelia couldn't shake a sliver of doubt—a feeling mirrored by Lady Grey. Perched on the window seat beside her, the cat scanned the landscape with a watchful alertness. Her ears twitched slightly, as though picking up a sound Amelia couldn't hear.

"He's just a guest," Amelia murmured, sipping her tea. "Maybe I'm looking for mysteries where there are none."

Lady Grey stretched lazily, her tail flicking dismissively, though her sharp gaze remained fixed on the horizon.

"Oh, don't look at me like that," Amelia said, smiling as she stroked the cat's fur. "We deserve a little peace and quiet, don't you think?"

The cat chirped softly, her expression skeptical, as though unconvinced by the suggestion.

Later that morning, Clara bustled into the parlor, her cheeks flushed from the brisk autumn wind. She carried a small stack of mail in one hand and a heavy bag of books in the other, balancing it all with practiced ease.

"Morning, Amelia," Clara greeted, dropping the mail onto the side table. "You'd think with the one mystery solved, things might slow down, but not in Tumblebrook."

"Always something to keep us on our toes," Amelia replied, setting down her empty teacup and moving to help Clara with the books.

Clara blew a strand of hair out of her face. "I popped by the historical society earlier. They're still sorting through the artifacts from the mine. They're planning an exhibit to honor Elias Carradine's work."

"That's wonderful," Amelia said warmly. "It's good to see something positive come out of all this. Gregor would have been pleased."

Clara nodded, her attention shifting to the stack of mail. As she sifted through the envelopes, her brow furrowed.

"What is it?" Amelia asked, noticing Clara's sudden focus.

Clara pulled out a thick, yellowed envelope. The paper looked old, its corners frayed as though it had been handled many times before. Across the front, Amelia's name was scrawled in an elegant but shaky script.

"This was in with the rest of the mail," Clara said, handing it to Amelia. "There's no return address or postmark. It looks like someone slipped it in."

Amelia took the envelope, its weight heavy in her hands. A faint earthy smell rose from it, as though it had been stored in an attic. Unease prickled at the back of her neck as she examined the handwriting.

"When did you pick this up?" she asked quietly.

"Just now," Clara said. "It was in the inn's mailbox with today's mail."

Amelia carefully opened the envelope, revealing a single sheet of paper. The handwriting inside matched the script on the envelope, deliberate and elegant.

Miss Farnsworth,

There are some things that cannot remain buried forever. History has a way of revealing itself when the time is right. Do not stop looking.

The answers you seek are in the shadows of the past.

Yours,

A Friend.

Amelia reread the note, its cryptic message leaving no doubt that whoever had written it knew far more than they were letting on.

"What does it say?" Clara asked, leaning closer.

Amelia handed her the note. "See for yourself."

Clara scanned the page, her frown deepening. "'The answers you seek are in the shadows of the past...' Amelia, do you think this has to do with the mine?"

"It feels deliberate," Amelia said, carefully folding the note.

"Whoever wrote this wanted me to find it. The question is why now? And what do they mean by 'history revealing itself'?"

Clara glanced toward the window, as though expecting to see someone lurking outside. "You don't think this has anything to do with Mr. Marlowe, do you?"

Amelia's expression darkened. "I don't know yet. But I'll be keeping an eye on him."

Clara hesitated. "I'm starting to think Tumblebrook's mysteries aren't quite ready to let us rest. What do we do now?"

Amelia smiled faintly. "We wait. Whoever sent this will reveal themselves eventually. And when they do, we'll be ready."

Lady Grey, who had been observing from her perch, let out a soft meow as though signaling her agreement.

That afternoon, Amelia was kneading dough in the kitchen when she heard footsteps. Dr. Westwood appeared, his leather satchel in hand, his expression as composed as ever.

"Leaving already?" Amelia asked, brushing flour from her hands.

Dr. Westwood nodded. "Duty calls. But I'll admit, Tumblebrook has left quite an impression on me."

"It tends to have that effect," Amelia said with a small smile. "Thank you for everything, Dr. Westwood. I'm not sure we could've done it without you."

"You give me too much credit," he replied. "Your instincts carried this investigation to its resolution." He paused, studying her carefully. "But I can't help feeling there's something unresolved here."

Amelia's smile faltered. "You're not the only one."

"Trust your instincts," he said firmly. "If there's more to uncover, I have no doubt you'll find it."

He opened his satchel and pulled out a small notebook. "I've made some notes—connections we might have missed. Keep this. It might prove useful."

Amelia accepted it, surprised. "Thank you."

As she walked him to the door, he turned before climbing into his car. "Good luck, Amelia. And take care of Lady Grey."

"Always," she replied.

As the car disappeared, Amelia flipped through the notebook. One phrase stood out: **What else lies buried in Tumblebrook?**

She glanced at Lady Grey, who had appeared silently by her side.

"Looks like we're not done yet, Lady."

The cat stared back, tail flicking, as though she too could sense the shadows still lingering.

Chapter 13

A Looming Secret

Clara tapped her pencil against the edge of her notebook, the rhythmic sound blending with the faint ticking of the antique clock in her bookstore. The cryptic letter addressed to Amelia lingered in her mind: *The answers you seek are in the shadows of the past.* Its message gnawed at her, insistently demanding attention.

Lady Grey lounged atop a stack of books nearby, her tail flicking lazily as if unimpressed by Clara's efforts. Clara glanced at the cat and sighed. "Well, Lady, it's not like the answers are going to jump out and introduce themselves."

The cat blinked slowly, amber eyes unwavering, as if to say, *Keep at it.*

Clara shook her head, frustration mounting. She had spent the morning scribbling down theories and tenuous connections, yet nothing seemed to fit. Who had sent the letter? Why now? And what exactly were the "shadows of the past"? For all her love of puzzles, this one felt maddeningly incomplete.

Suddenly, an idea struck. If the letter was rooted in Tumblebrook's history, there might be clues in the town's archives. With renewed determination, she grabbed the letter and made her way to the Tumblebrook Historical Society.

* * *

The society's ivy-covered brick headquarters exuded an air of timelessness, its quiet halls steeped in the scent of old paper and varnished wood. Inside, Mrs. Penelope Hargrove, the society's meticulous curator, looked up from her desk, peering over half-moon glasses.

"Good morning, Clara," Mrs. Hargrove greeted warmly. "Here to dig through the archives again?"

"Morning, Penelope. Actually, I was hoping you could help me with something specific today," Clara said, pulling the mysterious letter from her bag. "I'm trying to trace the origins of this."

Mrs. Hargrove took the letter carefully, her brow furrowing as she examined the aged paper. "This is quite old. The handwriting... it has a certain familiarity. Where did you find it?"

"It was delivered to the Lakeside Inn," Clara explained. "But it doesn't have a postmark, and none of us recognize the handwriting."

Mrs. Hargrove adjusted her glasses, leaning in closer. "The style is reminiscent of early 20th-century correspondence—formal, deliberate. The kind of penmanship taught in private schools or passed down in certain families. Wait here a moment."

She disappeared into the back room, leaving Clara alone with her thoughts. Lady Grey, who had slipped in unnoticed, prowled the room with quiet confidence, her ears twitching at every creak of the old building.

When Mrs. Hargrove returned, she carried a leather-bound ledger. "This is a record of local correspondences and documents from the early 1900s. Let's see if anything matches."

Together, they pored over the pages. Clara's pulse quickened when Mrs. Hargrove paused, her finger resting on an entry.

"Here we are," Mrs. Hargrove announced. "This handwriting... it's strikingly similar to that of Harriet Carradine."

"Elias Carradine's sister?" Clara asked, leaning in.

"Indeed," Mrs. Hargrove confirmed. "She corresponded frequently with Elias during his early years as an artist. Her letters often referenced his work and their shared family history."

Clara's mind raced. If the handwriting belonged to Harriet Carradine, why had a letter bearing her style surfaced now? Harriet had been dead for decades.

"Could someone in town be related to Harriet—someone who might have inherited her style of writing?" Clara asked.

Mrs. Hargrove tilted her head thoughtfully. "The Carradine family tree is... complicated. But we have records upstairs that might help clarify. Would you like me to retrieve them?"

"Please," Clara said, her curiosity growing.

* * *

Lady Grey trotted confidently across the town square, tail held high as though she carried the secrets of the Carradines herself. Clara followed the cat's deliberate path to the Carradine estate on the town's edge, its silhouette imposing against the fading afternoon light.

The estate, once grand, was now softened by neglect. Overgrown ivy clung to its stone walls, and the wrought-iron gates groaned as Clara pushed them open. Lady Grey slipped through a gap, her sleek form vanishing into the shadows.

Steeling herself, Clara followed. The front door creaked loudly as it opened, the sound reverberating through the stillness. Dust-coated furniture and faded wallpaper hinted at a place frozen in time, yet the house exuded an undeniable sense of expectation—almost as if it awaited their presence.

Lady Grey padded ahead, steps silent on the worn rug. Clara followed cautiously, her breath catching as she spotted a small table in the center of the room. On it lay a stack of papers, a photograph, and an envelope identical to the one delivered to Amelia.

Clara's heart raced. She approached the table, hands trembling as she picked up the photograph. Elias Carradine stood beside Harriet, their familial resemblance striking. But the young woman to their right—Evelyn—drew Clara's focus. Her bold features radiated quiet defiance, her presence commanding even in the static frame.

The room felt eerily still. As Clara reached for the papers, a creak from above froze her in place. Her eyes darted toward the ceiling. Lady Grey's ears twitched, and the cat let out a low growl, gaze fixed on the staircase.

"Who's there?" Clara called, voice trembling. The silence that followed was oppressive. After a moment, she exhaled shakily and turned back to the table.

Among the papers was a fragment of the Carradine family tree. Clara's eyes scanned the names, stopping abruptly at an unfamiliar entry: *Harriet Carradine – Daughter: Evelyn.*

"Evelyn?" Clara whispered. Why had her existence been erased from family records?

Lady Grey let out a soft chirp, drawing Clara's attention to the envelope. Its handwriting was unmistakable—identical to the letter addressed to Amelia. Clara opened it carefully, revealing another cryptic message:

The answers lie within these walls. Trust the keeper of the keys.

Clara's pulse quickened. The puzzle pieces were aligning, but the full picture remained elusive. Resolving to share her findings with Amelia, she tucked the photograph and papers into her bag.

As she turned to leave, a faint indentation on the dusty floorboards caught her eye. She crouched, brushing away the dirt to reveal a small metal ring embedded in the wood. It was a handle. Her breath caught as she realized it concealed a hidden hatch.

"Lady," Clara murmured, glancing at the cat. "You've led me to something big."

With a deep breath, Clara tugged on the ring. The hatch groaned as it opened, revealing a narrow staircase descending into darkness. A musty smell wafted upward. Clara's heart pounded, but she forced herself to peer into the shadows below.

"We'll come back," Clara whispered, closing the hatch carefully. "We need Amelia for this."

Lady Grey seemed to nod in agreement, tail swishing as they left the estate together.

Back at the Lakeside Inn, Clara entered the parlor as the sun dipped low on the horizon, casting a warm orange glow. Amelia looked up from Dr. Westwood's notebook, her brow furrowing at Clara's flustered expression.

"What happened?" Amelia asked, setting the notebook aside.

"You won't believe what I found," Clara began, placing the photograph and papers on the coffee table. She recounted her visit to the Carradine estate and the startling discovery of Evelyn Carradine's name.

Amelia's eyes widened as she examined the photograph. "Evelyn... why would her existence be hidden? This changes everything."

Lady Grey leapt onto the arm of the chair, her tail flicking as she watched the two women. Clara glanced at the cat, then back at Amelia.

"Whoever left that letter knew about Evelyn," Clara said firmly. "And they wanted us to find her story. The question is... why now?"

Amelia nodded, her mind already racing. "We need to dig deeper. This isn't just about the past—it's about how it's still affecting the present."

Chapter 14

Unearthed Connections

Amelia Farnsworth stood in the cozy parlor of the Lakeside Inn, staring at the aged photograph Clara brought back from the Carradine estate. The sepia tones lent it a haunting quality, the subjects frozen in time. In the center stood Elias Carradine, his expression proud yet somber, one hand resting on Harriet Carradine's shoulder. But it was the figure to the side—a young woman with striking features—that captured Amelia's focus. Faintly written on the back was a single name: *Evelyn.*

Dr. Jonathan Westwood leaned over her shoulder; his brow furrowed in thought. He had returned to the inn earlier that morning, drawn by Clara's discovery.

"This photograph," he said, his tone contemplative, "isn't just a family keepsake. It's a piece of a much larger puzzle."

Amelia nodded, her mind racing. "Evelyn Carradine. Why would her name be erased from family records? And why does her presence feel so... pivotal?"

Dr. Westwood tapped his chin. "Harriet's letters mentioned Evelyn sparingly, almost in passing. It's as though someone went to great lengths to ensure she was forgotten."

Amelia glanced at Lady Grey, perched gracefully on the arm of a nearby chair, her amber eyes fixed on the photograph. The cat's tail swished rhythmically, as though she, too, understood the significance of this discovery.

"Clara mentioned finding a hidden hatch at the estate," Amelia said. "She wanted to wait for us before exploring further. If Evelyn left behind anything—anything that explains her disappearance—it could be down there."

Dr. Westwood nodded. "We'll investigate after the festival closes down tonight. But keep in mind: the Carradine legacy is deeply rooted in Tumblebrook. There may still be people in town who know more than they've admitted."

Amelia placed the photograph on the coffee table, her shoulders heavy with unanswered questions. "Do you think the truth will change how Tumblebrook sees the Carradines?"

Dr. Westwood's expression softened. "History evolves, Amelia. The truth doesn't erase the past, but it reframes it. The Carradines have left an indelible mark on this town. Whatever we uncover might add complexity to their story, but it won't diminish their importance."

Amelia tilted her head thoughtfully. "Elias and Harriet poured so much into their art and this community. Evelyn feels like the missing piece—the part of their story that didn't quite fit."

Dr. Westwood leaned forward, resting his elbows on his knees. "And that's exactly why her story matters. What we've seen so far suggests Evelyn's role was pivotal—not just to her family but to something larger."

Amelia allowed herself a faint smile. "You're right. It's just that Tumblebrook's layers feel endless. You peel one back, and there's always another."

Dr. Westwood chuckled lightly. "That's why it takes someone with your intuition to navigate them. You see what others miss."

Amelia flushed slightly but quickly regained focus. "And you have the expertise to make sense of what I find. I suppose that makes us a good team."

Dr. Westwood smiled. "An effective one, I'd say. Now, let's ensure we're ready. Evelyn's story feels like the key to everything."

The late-afternoon sun cast a warm glow over Tumblebrook as townsfolk gathered in the square for the festival's banquet. Long tables lined the cobblestone streets, decorated with autumnal garlands and laden with local dishes. Laughter and lively conversation filled the air, a stark contrast to the undercurrent of secrets Amelia had been unraveling.

Amelia moved through the crowd, exchanging pleasantries and polite smiles, though her thoughts remained fixed on Evelyn Carradine. Someone here—someone in this square—might hold a fragment of the truth.

"Amelia!"

The familiar voice of Henry Biggs, the town's retired schoolteacher, called out. Amelia turned to see him seated on a bench, waving her over.

"Henry," she greeted warmly. "How have you been?"

Henry chuckled, his face crinkling with ease. "Oh, keeping busy as always. I hear you've been delving into Carradine history. Fascinating family, aren't they?"

Amelia raised an eyebrow. "What makes you say that?"

Henry leaned in conspiratorially, his tone lowering. "I knew Evelyn, you know. Long before she left Tumblebrook. Bright young woman, full of ideas. But there was always a sense of... conflict around her. Like she carried the weight of something bigger than herself."

Amelia's heart quickened. "What do you mean by conflict?"

Henry hesitated, his gaze growing distant. "Evelyn had a way of attracting attention—some good, some bad. She and Elias were close, but their relationship had... complications. And Harriet, well, she was fiercely protective of Evelyn. Maybe too much."

"You mean Harriet was overbearing?" Amelia pressed.

Henry nodded. "Yes, in her way. She wanted Evelyn to embrace the Carradine legacy, but Evelyn... she had her own vision. One that went far beyond what this town could offer."

"And the townspeople?" Amelia asked. "How did they see her?"

Henry's voice softened, tinged with memory. "With respect, mostly. But there was unease, too. Evelyn's ambition set her apart. Some admired it; others feared it. And there were whispers—about her influence on Elias. They said she inspired him in ways no one else could. She understood him more than Harriet ever did."

Amelia's thoughts raced. "Do you think Evelyn's departure was tied to Elias's art? Could it have been something she knew—or something they created together?"

Henry frowned. "It's possible. His work changed after she left—darker, more introspective. Some said it was grief. Maybe guilt." \

Dr. Westwood, who had joined them quietly, interjected. "Guilt over what?"

Henry glanced at him, hesitating. "A secret. One Evelyn might have taken with her."

* * *

As dusk descended, Amelia and Dr. Westwood excused themselves from the banquet and met Clara at the gate of the Carradine estate. Her excitement was tempered by a hint of apprehension.

"The hatch is just inside," Clara said, leading them down the overgrown path. Lady Grey trotted ahead, her movements purposeful.

Inside the estate, they found the hidden hatch exactly as Clara had described. Together, they lifted it, revealing a narrow staircase descending into darkness. A faint musty smell wafted upward, thick with the weight of years.

Amelia led the way, her flashlight casting flickering beams against the walls. At the bottom, they found a small, dimly lit room. Shelves lined the walls, filled with journals, letters, and artifacts that appeared untouched for decades. In the center of the room sat a wooden chest, its surface etched with intricate carvings.

Amelia knelt beside it, her hands trembling as she opened the lid. Inside were photographs, a stack of letters tied with a faded ribbon, and a leather-bound journal. Carefully, she lifted the journal and opened it to the first page.

Property of Evelyn Carradine, it read in elegant script.

Amelia's breath caught. "This is it," she whispered. "Her story. Everything she wanted us to find."

Dr. Westwood placed a hand on her shoulder. "We've reached the heart of the mystery, Amelia. Now we need to piece it together."

As they began to sift through the contents of the chest, Lady Grey sat silently nearby, her watchful eyes glinting in the faint light. The shadows of the past were finally coming to light, and Amelia knew they were on the brink of uncovering a truth that could reshape everything.

Chapter 15

Festival Under Strain

Dr. Jonathan Westwood strolled through the bustling festival square, his sharp eyes scanning the vibrant scene. The warm autumn sun bathed the cobblestone streets in a golden glow, and laughter echoed from the games section where children tossed rings and darted between stalls. Yet beneath the cheerful façade, he sensed a gnawing unease. Quick glances exchanged between council members, whispered conversations among vendors —signs of tension simmering beneath the surface.

As he passed the painting exhibition tent, a flash of movement caught his eye. Clara stood at the far end, clipboard in hand, gesturing animatedly toward a series of paintings displayed along the back wall. Her brow was furrowed, her usual calm replaced by a palpable urgency.

"Clara," he greeted, approaching with measured strides. "You look like someone on the verge of solving a puzzle—or unraveling one."

Clara turned, her expression tight. "Dr. Westwood, we might have a serious problem. Look at this."

She gestured to a large painting of Tumblebrook's lake at sunset.

At first glance, its vivid colors and delicate brushstrokes appeared to embody Elias Carradine's signature style. But as Dr. Westwood examined it more closely, subtle inconsistencies emerged.

"The technique is... off," he murmured, leaning closer. "The brushstrokes lack Carradine's precision. And the signature—it's slightly skewed."

Clara nodded, her voice low. "Exactly. I compared this to a verified Carradine painting. This one's a forgery."

Dr. Westwood straightened, his expression grim. "Passing off a forgery as an original during the festival isn't just unethical—it's a crime."

"And it gets worse," Clara added, glancing around to ensure they weren't overheard. "The painting was donated by Edith Cranston, one of the festival's main sponsors. If she's involved—or if someone's using this to frame her—it could ignite a scandal."

Dr. Westwood's eyes narrowed. "Have you spoken to Amelia about this yet?"

"Not yet," Clara admitted. "I wanted to confirm my suspicions first. But we need to bring her in. She has a way of cutting through the noise."

* * *

Amelia was engaged in a tense conversation with Councilman Dennis Griggs near the historical exhibit. His tone teetered between desperation and defensiveness as he gestured toward the display of artifacts from the recently unearthed Carradine estate.

"Amelia, you need to understand," Dennis implored. "This town's reputation is at stake. If any damaging information about the Carradine family comes out, it could ruin the festival's legacy—and ours."

Amelia remained calm, her gaze steady but unyielding. "Dennis, the truth isn't something we can bury to protect reputations. The townsfolk deserve honesty, even if it's uncomfortable."

Dennis sighed, running a hand through his graying hair. "You don't understand the pressure I'm under. The council is split. Half of them want to suppress anything controversial, while the others think transparency will win back the town's trust."

"And where do you stand, Dennis?" Amelia asked, her tone sharp but measured. "Are you with the half that wants to keep secrets?"

Dennis hesitated, his eyes darting toward the artifacts on display. "It's not that simple," he said finally. "My job is to maintain stability. If the Carradine family's skeletons come tumbling out, it'll divide the town. People will take sides, questioning every decision the council's made. Do you know what that would do to our tourism?"

Amelia folded her arms. "And what happens when those secrets come out anyway? Cover-ups always backfire. Transparency might hurt now, but it's better than a scandal later."

Dennis rubbed his temples, his shoulders slumping. "I just... I need more time. There are complications you don't understand."

"Then explain them to me," Amelia pressed. "If you want my help, I need to know what you're hiding."

Dennis leaned in, his voice dropping. "There's a document in the Carradine archives. It's not just about the family—it implicates people still living in Tumblebrook. Decisions were made years ago that shaped this town, and not all of them were ethical. If that document surfaces, it won't just damage the Carradine name—it'll destroy the people who built this community."

Amelia's eyes narrowed. "So this is about protecting individuals, not just the town's reputation."

Dennis straightened defensively. "Those individuals are the foundation of this town. They made sacrifices—did what they thought was best at the time."

"Even if it wasn't right?" she countered.

Dennis flinched but remained silent. The weight of his omission hung between them.

Before Amelia could press further, Dr. Westwood and Clara

approached, their expressions urgent. Sensing their mood, Amelia turned to them immediately. "What's happened?"

"We've found a forged painting in the Carradine exhibition," Dr. Westwood said, his tone brisk. "It's being displayed as an original."

Amelia's eyes widened. "A forgery? Do we know who's responsible?"

Clara shook her head. "Not yet. But the painting was donated by Edith Cranston. If she's aware it's a fake, that's one thing. If she's not..." She let the implication hang in the air.

Amelia glanced at Dennis, who had gone pale. "Dennis, do you know anything about this?"

"No, of course not," Dennis stammered. "But if Edith is involved —or if someone's trying to frame her—this could be disastrous."

"We need to confront Edith," Amelia said decisively. "Dr. Westwood, Clara, come with me. Dennis, stay here and keep an eye on the exhibit. If word of the forgery spreads, we'll have chaos."

* * *

They found Edith near the festival's central pavilion, chatting with a group of local artists. Her expression brightened as they approached.

"Amelia, Dr. Westwood, Clara," she greeted warmly. "Enjoying the festival?"

Amelia didn't waste time. "Edith, we need to speak with you about a painting you donated to the exhibition."

Edith's smile faltered. "Is something wrong?"

Dr. Westwood stepped forward. "We've discovered that one of the paintings attributed to Elias Carradine is a forgery. We need to know where it came from."

Edith's face drained of color. "A forgery? That's impossible. That painting has been in my family for decades. It was passed down from my grandmother, who was close friends with the Carradines."

Clara's voice was gentle. "Edith, it's possible you've been misled. Forgers are skilled, and even family heirlooms can turn out to be fakes. We're not accusing you of anything—we just want to understand."

Edith clutched her hands together, visibly shaken. "I... I would never knowingly display a forgery. You have to believe me."

Amelia placed a reassuring hand on her arm. "We do. But we need your help. Could anyone else in your family have handled the painting before it came to you?"

Edith frowned in thought. "My mother once mentioned my grandfather acquired it through a private auction. If there was deception, it might have happened then."

Dr. Westwood nodded. "Do you have any records of the transaction? Even a name or location could help."

Edith's expression brightened slightly. "I think there's a ledger in my office. I'll look for it as soon as the festival concludes."

Clara offered a warm smile. "That would be incredibly helpful. We're not here to accuse you, Edith—we just want to protect the integrity of the exhibit."

Edith exhaled slowly. "Thank you. I'll do whatever I can."

As the festival continued, the strain among officials grew more apparent. Whispers circulated through the crowd, and the festive atmosphere became increasingly brittle. Back at the Lakeside Inn, Amelia, Dr. Westwood, and Clara convened around the dining room table.

"The forgery, the Carradine family secrets, the council's divisions..." Amelia said, her voice heavy. "Everything points to something much bigger."

Dr. Westwood nodded, his tone resolute. "We're on the verge of uncovering the truth. But whoever's behind this isn't going to let it come to light easily."

Amelia's gaze hardened. "Then we'll be ready. Tumblebrook deserves the truth, no matter how difficult it is to face."

Lady Grey leapt onto the table, her amber eyes glinting with quiet understanding. The room fell silent, a sense of resolve settling over them. The shadows of the past were closer than ever, and it was time to bring them into the light.

Chapter 16

An Unexpected Ally

Amelia Farnsworth sat at the dining room table of the Lakeside Inn, her gaze fixed on the scattered notes and papers in front of her. The rhythmic patter of rain against the window added to the tension in the room. Across from her, Dr. Jonathan Westwood scribbled in his leather-bound journal, occasionally glancing up as though waiting for her to speak.

"It feels like the pieces are all here," Amelia said finally, her voice laced with frustration. "We're just not seeing how they fit together."

Dr. Westwood paused, tapping his pen against the table. "The forgery, the council's secrets, Evelyn Carradine's disappearance... they're connected. I'm certain of it. But there's still something we're missing."

Their conversation was interrupted by a firm knock at the front door. Amelia frowned, glancing at the clock. It was late for visitors.

"I'll get it," she said, rising from her chair.

When she opened the door, Edith Cranston stood on the porch, clutching an umbrella that dripped rainwater onto the steps. Her usual composed demeanor was replaced by visible distress.

"Edith," Amelia said, stepping aside to let her in. "Come in—you're soaked."

Edith entered quickly, her heels clicking against the wooden floor. "I'm sorry to intrude, but I need to talk to you. It's urgent."

Amelia exchanged a glance with Dr. Westwood before guiding Edith to the sitting room. Once seated, Edith clasped her hands tightly, her composure fraying.

"I've been thinking about what you said earlier about the painting," Edith began, her voice trembling. "And... there's something I haven't told you."

Amelia leaned forward, her expression steady. "Go on."

Edith hesitated, her gaze dropping to her hands. "The painting... it might not have come from my grandfather after all. I found a letter among my grandmother's belongings years ago. It hinted at something... personal. She might have had a relationship with Elias Carradine."

Dr. Westwood raised an eyebrow. "A relationship? Are you suggesting an affair?"

Edith nodded, her face flushed. "The letter implied as much. It said Elias gifted her the painting—something deeply personal. If that's true, it might explain why the style is different. It wasn't meant for public display."

Amelia's mind raced. "If the painting was personal, it makes sense that it wouldn't match his official works. But why would someone forge it now?"

"To discredit Edith or her family," Dr. Westwood suggested, his tone thoughtful. "If someone wanted to stir up doubt about her or the Carradines, this would be an effective way to do it. Edith, do you still have the letter?"

Edith's face fell. "I burned it years ago. I didn't want anyone finding it and tarnishing my family's name. But... there's something else. My grandmother once mentioned a hidden compartment at the Carradine estate. She said Elias kept personal items there. If it still exists, it could hold answers."

Amelia sat up straighter, her pulse quickening. "A hidden compartment? That might be the key we've been looking for."

* * *

Later that evening, Amelia, Dr. Westwood, and Lady Grey stood at the edge of the Carradine estate. The rain had ceased, leaving the air damp and thick with the scent of wet earth. Flashlights in hand, they navigated the overgrown garden, their breaths visible in the cool night air.

Lady Grey trotted ahead, her tail swishing confidently. Amelia couldn't help but smile at the cat's self-assured demeanor. "I swear, she knows exactly what we're looking for."

Dr. Westwood chuckled. "She's proven to have sharper instincts than most people. Let's trust her lead."

The cat paused near a crumbling stone wall, her eyes fixed on a narrow doorway half-hidden by ivy. She let out a soft meow, her ears twitching.

"This must be it," Amelia said, pushing open the heavy wooden door. It groaned on its hinges, revealing a dark, musty corridor lined with cobwebs.

They ventured inside, the narrow beam of their flashlights cutting through the gloom. The air grew colder as they moved deeper into the estate. At last, they entered a small room filled with forgotten furniture and crates draped in dust. In the center stood a large wooden desk.

Lady Grey leapt onto the desk, pawing at one of the drawers with deliberate intent. Amelia approached cautiously, noticing a faint seam along the bottom of the drawer.

"There's something hidden here," she said, carefully prying the bottom panel loose.

Inside was a leather-bound journal, its cover worn and cracked with age. Amelia opened it gently, her breath catching as she recognized the handwriting.

"It's Elias's journal," she whispered.

Dr. Westwood leaned closer, his expression intent. "Does it mention anything about Edith's grandmother?"

Amelia flipped through the brittle pages, scanning the entries. Her finger paused on a passage dated March 12, 1923.

I find myself drawn to her in ways I cannot explain. She sees the world as I do, through colors and emotions. I've gifted her one of my most personal works, a painting that captures the essence of our connection. It is not for the world to see, but for her alone.

Amelia looked up, her voice tinged with awe. "This confirms it. Elias and Edith's grandmother had a relationship. The painting wasn't meant for public display. But why would someone forge it now?"

Before Dr. Westwood could respond, Lady Grey let out a sharp meow, pawing at a corner of the room. Amelia knelt beside her, prying up a loose floorboard to reveal a small metal box. Inside were letters, photographs, and a delicate locket.

Amelia picked up one of the letters, her hands trembling as she read the opening line: *To my dearest Evelyn.*

Dr. Westwood's eyes widened. "Evelyn Carradine? Could this be the same Evelyn who disappeared?"

"It has to be," Amelia murmured, her mind racing. "This changes everything."

They sifted through the box's contents. The letters hinted at a secret relationship between Evelyn and someone referred to only as "R." A photograph showed Evelyn beside a man, his face partially obscured. Behind them stood a structure that didn't match anything on the estate map.

Dr. Westwood studied the photograph closely. "This looks like an old carriage house. If it still exists, it might hold more answers."

Amelia nodded. "We'll investigate it tomorrow. But for now, let's document everything."

As they exited the estate, Edith was waiting near the gate,

wringing her hands nervously. "Did you find anything?" she asked, her voice wavering.

Amelia hesitated before answering, her tone gentle but firm. "We found something significant. Evelyn's story isn't finished, Edith. And neither is Elias's."

Edith's eyes filled with unshed tears. "Thank you. Whatever happens, I need to know the truth."

Dr. Westwood stepped forward, his voice steady. "The truth is rarely simple, Edith. But it's always worth uncovering. We'll figure this out—together."

Edith squared her shoulders, determination flickering in her gaze. "I've spent my life believing the Carradines were the source of my family's pain. If there's more to the story, I need to know it—for myself and for my family."

Amelia placed a reassuring hand on Edith's arm. "We'll help you. But be prepared—the truth might not be what you expect."

Edith nodded, her voice resolute. "I'm ready. Whatever it is, I'm ready."

Chapter 17

Echoes of Betrayal

Clara sat at the kitchen table, sunlight streaming through the windows and pooling over the scattered artifacts and papers. The comforting scent of coffee mingled with the faint lavender of a burning candle—a feeble attempt to counterbalance the oppressive weight of the Carradine estate's secrets. The items before her felt less like a treasure trove and more like a labyrinth, and Clara was determined to find its center.

Lady Grey curled up on the chair beside her, her tail flicking occasionally as though responding to the tension in the room. Clara leaned back, tapping her pen against the edge of her notebook, which was already filled with scribbled questions and fragmented connections.

"What else were you hiding, Elias?" she murmured.

She returned to Elias Carradine's journal, carefully flipping through the brittle pages. The passage confirming Elias's connection to Edith's grandmother lingered in her mind, but the journal hinted at more than romance—it brimmed with guilt, frustration, and cryptic references to decisions made under duress. Clara scribbled a note in the margin of her notebook: *What decisions?*

Lady Grey stretched lazily, blinking up at Clara as though she held the answers. Clara chuckled faintly, scratching the cat's ears. "If only you could talk, Lady. I bet you'd have this sorted out in no time."

* * *

By mid-morning, Clara had relocated to the Tumblebrook Historical Society. The reading room smelled of varnished wood and aged paper, the air hushed save for the ticking of a grandfather clock. Lady Grey, true to form, perched on a nearby chair, her amber eyes scanning the room like a watchful assistant.

Clara was poring over a ledger from 1925 when a specific entry caught her attention: *"Land dispute settled in favor of Carradine family."* The notation suggested a legal battle with a rival party, though the lack of detail was frustrating. Her pulse quickened. *Who lost that dispute, and what did it cost them?*

Flipping further, she found a faded contract between the Carradine and Cranston families. At first glance, it detailed a partnership, but inconsistencies emerged as she read further—profit margins that didn't align, veiled references to withheld funds.

"So, it wasn't as amicable as everyone thought," Clara murmured, underlining key phrases in her notebook.

Lady Grey leapt gracefully from her perch, her paws landing on a low shelf. She batted at a book until it tipped over, revealing a slim, dusty ledger hidden beneath. Clara picked it up, brushing away the dust.

The ledger's cryptic financial entries used initials instead of full names, but one set—R.C.—recurred frequently alongside substantial payments. Clara's mind raced. *Richard Carradine. What were you funneling money into?*

Another letter surfaced, penned by Elias. Its tone was anxious, apologizing to a partner for financial discrepancies and blaming his brother, Richard, for mishandling funds.

"Richard again," Clara muttered, her pen moving swiftly across her notebook. "Everything points back to you."

Lady Grey chirped, pawing at a folded map that had slipped from a folder. Clara unfolded it to reveal the original layout of the Carradine estate. Several structures, long since demolished, were marked with stars. One, labeled *Storage Shed,* drew her attention.

"Good find, Lady," Clara said, tracing the map's lines. "This might be exactly what we need."

That evening, Clara reconvened with Amelia and Dr. Westwood at the Lakeside Inn. The dining room table, now their de facto war room, was cluttered with maps, papers, and notes. Lady Grey perched on a chair, her amber eyes following their every move.

"I found something big," Clara began, spreading her findings across the table. "The Carradines and Cranstons had a falling-out over land and finances. The betrayal was never resolved. If that grudge lingered through the years, it might explain why someone would target Edith now."

Dr. Westwood nodded, his expression thoughtful. "Grudges can last generations in small towns. Old wounds fester, and secrets only deepen them."

Amelia studied the map Clara had unearthed. "This *Storage Shed* might hold more than tools and forgotten furniture. If it's intact, it could connect the dots between the past and the present."

The decision was unanimous: they would investigate first thing in the morning.

* * *

The next day, the air was crisp, the scent of damp leaves accompanying Clara, Amelia, Dr. Westwood, and Lady Grey as they approached the overgrown grounds of the Carradine estate. Flashlights and tools in hand, they wove through the underbrush, the morning sun casting long shadows across the property.

Hidden behind a dense thicket, the storage shed was weathered and worn, its door secured by a rusted latch. Clara carefully pried it open, the creak of the hinges slicing through the still morning air.

Inside, the air was heavy with age and dust. Sunlight filtered through gaps in the wooden slats, illuminating crates and trunks stacked haphazardly. Lady Grey darted to a corner, her tail flicking as she sniffed the ground.

"Let's start with the crates," Amelia suggested, steadying her flashlight.

Dr. Westwood opened the first crate, revealing canvases wrapped in protective cloth. He unwrapped one, inhaling sharply. "These are unfinished works," he said, holding up a half-painted canvas. "Drafts of Elias's later pieces. This could change how historians view his career."

Clara uncovered a stack of ledgers in another crate. "These date back to the early 1900s," she said. "Elias wasn't just an artist. He was funding projects across town. But look at this—large sums of money are unaccounted for."

Amelia was drawn to a trunk in the corner. Using a crowbar, she pried it open to reveal a journal, a locket, and letters tied with a faded ribbon. As she flipped through the journal, her brow furrowed.

"Elias suspected his brother of sabotaging their family finances," Amelia said. "He believed Richard was using their name for personal gain."

"That matches the ledgers," Clara added. "Richard's actions could have created enemies far beyond their family."

Amelia picked up one of the letters, her breath catching at the salutation: *To my dearest Evelyn.*

Dr. Westwood leaned closer. "Evelyn Carradine? Could this explain her disappearance?"

Before Amelia could respond, Lady Grey let out a sharp meow, drawing their attention to a loose floorboard. Beneath it was a small metal box containing a deed for land outside Tumblebrook and a list of names—including several prominent families still living in town.

"This is it," Clara said, her voice hushed. "The link between past and present. Whoever holds this knowledge has leverage over the entire town."

As they left the shed, the weight of their discoveries pressed heavily upon them. The Carradine estate had revealed its secrets, but the implications stretched far beyond its crumbling walls. Betrayal, ambition, and long-held grudges had shaped Tumblebrook's history, and unearthing the truth would come at a cost.

"We're close," Amelia said, her voice resolute. "But this is bigger than I imagined. We need to tread carefully."

Dr. Westwood nodded. "The past never stays buried for long, and someone doesn't want us digging it up."

Clara glanced at Lady Grey, who seemed undeterred by the gravity of their findings. "Well," Clara said with a faint smile, "at least we have Lady Grey on our side."

Amelia's lips curved into a determined smile. "And that might just make all the difference."

Chapter 18

Beyond the Surface

Amelia Farnsworth stood at the edge of Tumblebrook's lake, the early morning mist clinging to the water like a spectral veil. The soft, damp soil beneath her boots shifted slightly, anchoring her in the present as she gazed out at the horizon. In her hand was the map Clara had unearthed, its edges frayed and annotations faint but legible. Each marked location represented a thread in the tangled web of the Carradine mystery. Today, Amelia intended to follow those threads—wherever they led.

* * *

The Griggs estate loomed before her, its manicured hedges and pristine flowerbeds presenting a veneer of order that contrasted sharply with the chaos Amelia suspected lay beneath. Dennis Griggs opened the door, his expression equal parts surprise and wariness.

"Amelia," he greeted, stepping aside to let her in. "To what do I owe this early visit?"

"I'm hoping you can help me," Amelia said, offering a polite smile as she stepped into the familiar warmth of his home. "I need to

96

understand more about the Carradine family—and their connections to Tumblebrook's past."

Dennis's brows furrowed as he led her into his study. The room smelled faintly of pipe tobacco, its shelves lined with leather-bound volumes and neatly arranged artifacts. He gestured for her to sit, settling into his armchair across from her.

"You've always had a knack for finding trouble," Dennis said lightly, though his tone carried an edge of unease. "What is it this time?"

Amelia unfolded the map and placed it on the table between them. "This map outlines the original layout of the Carradine estate," she began, pointing to one of the marked locations. "We've already found evidence of financial transactions involving the Griggs family in one of these structures."

Dennis stiffened, his jaw tightening. "That was a long time ago," he said tersely. "Whatever dealings my grandfather had with the Carradines are ancient history."

"Are they?" Amelia asked, her tone calm but insistent. "Land disputes, missing funds, accusations of betrayal—those patterns seem to be resurfacing now. And someone is using them to disrupt the festival."

Dennis leaned back, clasping his hands tightly in his lap. For a long moment, he said nothing, his gaze fixed on the map. Finally, he exhaled heavily. "There's a ledger," he admitted, his voice low. "My grandfather kept detailed records of his dealings with the Carradines. It's buried somewhere in the estate archives."

Amelia leaned forward, her heart quickening. "What kind of information does it contain?"

Dennis hesitated. "Not just financial records," he said. "There were agreements—informal, often unspoken—between families. Some were aboveboard, but others... weren't. If the wrong person got their hands on that ledger, it could ruin reputations that have taken generations to build."

"That's exactly why we need to see it," Amelia said firmly. "This isn't just about the past, Dennis. It's about protecting the future of this town. The festival, Tumblebrook's unity—everything is at stake."

After a long pause, Dennis gave a reluctant nod. "I'll search for it tonight. Meet me back here tomorrow, and I'll let you know what I find."

* * *

Edith greeted Amelia on the porch, her demeanor calmer than it had been the day before. Inside, the air was warm and inviting, scented with lemon cookies and freshly brewed tea.

"I've been thinking about what we discussed," Edith said once they were seated in the parlor. Her hands trembled slightly as she poured tea, betraying her underlying nerves. "There's something I haven't told you."

Amelia set her cup down, her curiosity piqued. "I'm listening."

Edith reached for a small wooden box on the coffee table. From it, she retrieved a delicate gold locket, its chain glinting in the sunlight. She handed it to Amelia, who opened it carefully. Inside was a tiny portrait of a young woman who bore a striking resemblance to Edith, alongside a man whose features were unmistakably Carradine.

"That's my grandmother, Margaret Cranston, and Elias Carradine," Edith said softly. "I found the locket among her belongings after she passed. She never spoke about him, but I remember her staring at this locket as if it held the answers to a question she couldn't ask."

Amelia turned the locket over, her thumb brushing against an inscription etched into the back: *To M., with all my heart.*

"This inscription," Amelia murmured. "It matches one of the letters we found in the storage shed. Elias wrote it to someone he called 'M.'"

Edith's expression tightened. "I've always believed my grandmother loved Elias, but she never spoke of it. Perhaps she was protecting him—or herself—from Richard's wrath. He had a reputation for being ruthless, even within the family."

Amelia nodded thoughtfully. "If Margaret knew about Richard's schemes, she might have hidden this to protect Elias's legacy. But why keep it a secret all these years?"

Edith's hands tightened around her teacup. "Because secrets are the currency of Tumblebrook," she said bitterly. "Revealing the truth would have come at a cost my grandmother wasn't willing to pay."

Amelia placed the locket gently on the table. "Thank you for trusting me with this, Edith. It's another piece of the puzzle, but we still have more to uncover."

Amelia returned to the Lakeside Inn that evening, where Clara and Dr. Westwood were waiting. The dining room table, as always, was a battlefield of maps, letters, and photographs. Lady Grey perched atop a stack of books, her amber eyes watchful.

Amelia recounted her conversations with Dennis and Edith, placing the locket on the table as she spoke. Clara's eyes lit up with recognition as she examined it.

"This confirms Margaret Cranston was the 'M.' in Elias's letters," Clara said. "But it also means their connection was more than just romantic—it was integral to the tensions within the Carradine family."

Dr. Westwood nodded. "And if Richard saw Margaret as a threat to his control, he could have gone to great lengths to discredit or silence her."

Clara traced her finger over the map. "We need to investigate the other marked locations. If there are more hidden spaces like the storage shed, they could hold the answers we're missing."

Amelia agreed, her resolve hardening. "Tomorrow, we dig deeper. Someone is using these old secrets to manipulate the present, and we need to figure out who—and why."

Lady Grey stretched languidly, then hopped off her perch to nudge the locket with her paw. Amelia smiled faintly. "Looks like we've got her approval."

As the room fell into thoughtful silence, the weight of the mystery hung heavily in the air. Amelia glanced at her companions, their determination matching her own. Together, they would untangle Tumblebrook's web of lies—no matter what awaited them.

Chapter 19

The Unexpected Opening

The morning dawned crisp and cold, the first hints of frost painting the edges of the windowpanes at the Lakeside Inn. In the dining room, Amelia Farnsworth surveyed the cluttered table before her—a patchwork of maps, ledgers, and fragile artifacts that offered pieces of a puzzle yet to be solved. The fire in the hearth crackled steadily, its warmth contrasting with the chill of the autumn air outside.

Clara sat across from Amelia, a steaming mug of tea untouched by her side. Her dark hair framed her face as she hunched over a ledger, the weariness in her eyes tempered by determination. Lady Grey, as ever, perched nearby, her tail flicking in time with Clara's pencil tapping against the table.

"Do you think we've gathered everything we need?" Clara asked, setting the pencil down and rubbing her temples. "Every clue seems to unravel into more questions."

Amelia allowed herself a faint smile, though her tone remained pragmatic. "That's the nature of this kind of work—every thread we pull uncovers another tangle."

The sound of approaching footsteps on the staircase brought

their attention to Dr. Westwood. His leather satchel hung casually from one shoulder, and his calm, measured expression belied the urgency of the situation.

"Good morning," he greeted, his voice steady. "I've been reviewing the sketches from the carriage house. If those coordinates are accurate, we might finally uncover something definitive."

Clara slid the ledger toward him. "I've been poring over these financial records again. There's a clear pattern of missing funds and misattributed projects. Someone went to great lengths to hide the trail."

Amelia's tone sharpened slightly. "And every lead points back to Richard Carradine. He wasn't just hiding money—he was orchestrating something on a much larger scale."

Dr. Westwood nodded thoughtfully, flipping through the ledger. "If this was about control, influence, or a deeper betrayal, the answers could lie at the location marked by those coordinates. But we should also be prepared for resistance. Whoever's behind this won't let us uncover the truth easily."

Lady Grey leapt onto the table, her amber eyes narrowing as her paw rested on the map, directing attention to a marked spot. Amelia chuckled softly, scratching the cat's ears.

"She's pointing us in the right direction again," Amelia said with a faint smile.

Dr. Westwood smirked. "A cat's intuition is often underestimated."

Clara leaned back, her pencil now tapping against her notebook. "Don't forget, we also have the historical society's unveiling this afternoon. If someone's been trying to keep these secrets buried, they'll be watching that event closely."

Amelia nodded, her resolve hardening. "Then we split our efforts. Before the unveiling, we'll check the carriage house. If the coordinates match, there might be something we've missed."

* * *

The carriage house stood at the edge of the Carradine estate, obscured by overgrown brush and tall oaks. The once-proud structure leaned under the weight of neglect, its weathered walls and sagging roof bearing the scars of time.

Amelia, Clara, and Dr. Westwood approached cautiously, their flashlights cutting through the dim morning light. Lady Grey trotted ahead, slipping through a gap in the doorway with a soft meow.

"This place looks like it's held together by willpower," Clara muttered, inspecting the splintered doorframe.

Inside, the air was damp and heavy with the scent of decay. Beams of light filtered through cracks in the walls, illuminating piles of rusted tools and warped wood. Crates stacked in the corners hinted at a time when this space had been meticulously maintained.

"Storage, most likely," Dr. Westwood remarked, stepping carefully over debris. "But if the coordinates are correct, there's something more hidden here."

Lady Grey's low growl drew their attention to a corner of the room. The cat pawed at a section of floorboards, her tail flicking with insistence.

"What is it, Lady?" Amelia crouched beside her, knocking lightly on the boards. The hollow sound beneath confirmed her suspicions. "There's a compartment here."

Dr. Westwood retrieved a crowbar from his satchel and worked it beneath the edge of the boards. With a groan of old wood, the hidden space was revealed, and inside lay bundles wrapped in oilcloth. Clara unwrapped the first bundle, revealing a ledger filled with dense, handwritten entries.

"Financial records," she said, her voice low with realization. "These document more missing funds—and more names. Richard Carradine is tied to nearly every entry."

Amelia unfolded a brittle letter from the cache, her hands steady as she read aloud: *To my dearest Richard, you must ensure our plans remain hidden. Elias cannot know what we've done, nor can the others. The family's reputation depends on it.*

Clara's breath caught. "This wasn't just about money," she whispered. "It was about consolidating power and silencing dissent. And Richard wasn't working alone."

Dr. Westwood's expression darkened. "Look here—initials at the bottom of the letter. H.G. Henry Griggs."

Amelia's eyes narrowed. "So the Griggs family wasn't just collateral damage in this feud—they were active participants."

* * *

The historical society's main hall buzzed with anticipation as townsfolk gathered for the unveiling. The hum of conversation filled the space, but Amelia couldn't ignore the tension that hung in the air. Her eyes scanned the crowd, landing on Edith Cranston, who appeared unusually subdued, and Dennis Griggs, lingering near the refreshment table with a guarded posture.

The event began with Mrs. Hargrove delivering a speech on the importance of preserving Tumblebrook's history. Polite applause followed as the first artifact—a ledger from the Carradine archives—was revealed.

Amelia's gaze shifted to a figure near the back of the room. The man's presence was incongruous—his piercing eyes fixed on the display, his demeanor more calculating than curious.

"Do you recognize him?" Clara whispered, following Amelia's line of sight.

Amelia shook her head. "No. But he's not here for the history."

Dr. Westwood's gaze darkened as he observed the man. "We'll keep a close watch on him."

As the rain began to lash against the windows, the storm outside echoed the charged atmosphere within the hall. The unveiling of the Carradine artifacts had drawn out not just the curious but those desperate to keep secrets buried.

That evening, back at the Lakeside Inn, the trio sifted through the recovered documents from the carriage house. Clara traced the faint symbols etched into one of Elias Carradine's sketches, her mind racing with possibilities.

"These symbols could be coordinates—or a cipher," she said. "If we decode them, they might lead us to the heart of this conspiracy."

Amelia nodded. "And likely to the secrets Richard fought to protect. If we're going to find the truth, this is the trail we need to follow."

Dr. Westwood's voice was steady, resolute. "But we should proceed carefully. The storm outside is nothing compared to what's brewing in this town."

Lady Grey meowed softly, her amber eyes reflecting the flickering firelight. Amelia reached out, scratching behind the cat's ears. "Don't worry, Lady. We'll find the answers—and make sure the truth sees the light of day."

As they prepared for the final stretch of their investigation, the weight of Tumblebrook's hidden history pressed heavily on them. Yet in that moment, a shared determination bound them together. The past wouldn't remain buried much longer.

Chapter 20

Hesitant Revelations

The early morning light filtered through the dining room of the Lakeside Inn, casting a soft glow over the organized chaos of maps, sketches, and letters spread across the wooden table. Amelia Farnsworth paced slowly, her boots tapping rhythmically against the floorboards as her mind worked to connect the fragmented pieces of the Carradine puzzle. Despite the fire crackling in the hearth, a chill lingered in the air, a quiet echo of the weight they all felt.

Clara sat hunched over the table, her pencil tapping against her notebook. Notes filled the pages before her in a whirlwind of thoughts and observations. She tilted a sketch toward the sunlight streaming through the window, her brow furrowed in concentration. Lady Grey perched serenely on the windowsill, her tail swishing with measured deliberation, as if she too were puzzling through the mystery.

"These symbols aren't random," Clara said, her voice breaking the stillness. She tilted the sketch again, her gaze sharp. "Elias must have created them with intention—something tied to the estate, or maybe the geography of the town itself."

Dr. Westwood, seated at the head of the table, tapped his pen against a worn ledger. His coffee sat untouched, its steam curling upward and dissipating. "The coordinates suggest a specific location, possibly within walking distance of the estate. If it's another hidden cache, it might hold the answers we've been chasing."

Amelia paused her pacing, her gaze snapping to the map pinned to the table. "What if the symbols are a grid system? This wooded area near the old mining road aligns with the coordinates—and it's remote enough for Elias to have hidden something there."

Lady Grey leapt from the windowsill to the table with feline precision, her paw landing squarely on the very spot Amelia had indicated. She looked up with a soft meow, her amber eyes unwavering, as if affirming the choice.

Clara let out a breathy laugh, her lips curving into a faint smile. "Looks like Lady Grey's officially our guide."

Dr. Westwood chuckled, his earlier seriousness giving way to a moment of levity. "We'd be foolish not to trust her instincts at this point."

Amelia glanced at Lady Grey, a wry smile tugging at her lips. "She's been right so far. Who am I to argue?"

Lady Grey circled the map once before settling near the edge, her eyes bright with unspoken understanding. Dr. Westwood leaned forward, his tone turning resolute. "If Lady Grey's confident, I say we follow her lead. Let's check the site before the historical society's unveiling. The more we uncover now, the better prepared we'll be for what's coming."

The group exchanged a determined glance. The truth about the Carradine family—and Tumblebrook's buried secrets—lay within their reach.

* * *

The trail to the suspected location wound through dense forest, the underbrush thick with damp leaves and twisting roots. Amelia led the way, her flashlight cutting through the low morning mist. Behind her, Clara followed closely, the map clutched in her hands, while Dr. Westwood brought up the rear, his satchel swaying with each step.

"This area hasn't been touched in decades," Amelia murmured, her voice soft, blending into the forest's natural quiet. "If Elias left something here, it's likely untouched."

The path narrowed as the trees pressed closer, their branches intertwining overhead to form a natural canopy. The earthy scent of moss and decaying leaves filled the air. Lady Grey darted ahead, her gray coat blending with the shadows. She stopped abruptly near a small clearing, her ears pricking and her tail flicking with purpose.

"This feels different," Clara remarked as they stepped into the clearing. The trees opened slightly, revealing a serene space where the faint sound of trickling water mingled with the rustling of leaves. At the center of the clearing stood a moss-covered stone marker, half-buried under layers of fallen foliage.

"There's something engraved here," Clara said, brushing away the moss. Her fingers traced faint words carved into the stone: *To those who seek, the truth awaits.*

Dr. Westwood stepped closer, his expression sharpening. "Elias left this as a guide. Whatever we're looking for must be nearby."

Amelia's flashlight caught the glint of something metallic near the base of the marker. She crouched, brushing away the dirt to reveal a lockbox, its hinges worn with age. Her companions gathered around as she carefully pried it open. Inside, a journal, a rolled-up canvas, and a bundle of letters tied with a faded ribbon awaited them.

Amelia lifted the journal, its leather cover cracked with age. She read the inscription on the first page aloud, her voice barely above a whisper: "*This journal belongs to Elias Carradine. To those who find it, may you understand the burden of truth and the cost of secrets.*"

Clara untied the ribbon from the letters, her voice steady as she read the addressee. "Margaret Cranston. This confirms Edith's grandmother was deeply tied to Elias."

Dr. Westwood unrolled the canvas, revealing a painting that sent a collective shiver through the group. It depicted the Carradine estate, but in the foreground loomed a shadowy figure, its indistinct form radiating an aura of menace.

"This isn't just a painting," Dr. Westwood said, his voice grave. "It's a warning. Elias wasn't just documenting his art—he was leaving a message about the dangers he faced."

Amelia turned her attention back to the journal, her fingers lingering on its weathered pages. "Elias knew this day would come," she murmured. "He wanted this to be found."

The wind stirred the clearing, rustling the leaves. Lady Grey circled the lockbox, her amber eyes reflecting the faint light filtering through the canopy. The group packed the items carefully, their collective resolve strengthening as they prepared to unravel the Carradine family's final secrets.

Back at the Lakeside Inn, the trio pored over their discoveries in the dining room. The space hummed with focused energy, the table overflowing with artifacts and documents. Clara typed furiously on her laptop, cross-referencing entries in Elias's journal with old town records. Dr. Westwood scrutinized the painting with a magnifying glass, his brow furrowed in thought.

"These entries suggest Richard wasn't just exploiting the family for financial gain," Clara said, her voice steady but tinged with disbelief. "He was actively sabotaging Elias to consolidate control."

Amelia held one of Margaret Cranston's letters, her fingers brushing over the ink. "Margaret wasn't just a confidante. She was Elias's anchor. He trusted her with everything."

Dr. Westwood leaned back, his expression darkening. "This shadowy figure in the painting—it might represent Richard. But look here." He pointed to a faint inscription at the painting's corner: *He watches but cannot erase.*

"Elias refused to be silenced," Amelia said, her voice firm. "Even in the face of betrayal."

Lady Grey leapt onto the table, her paw landing near the journal. Her gaze seemed to challenge them, urging them onward.

"The truth might be painful," Clara said quietly. "But it's better than letting these lies fester."

Amelia's eyes blazed with determination. "Then we reveal everything. Tumblebrook deserves to know the truth—no matter what it costs."

Dr. Westwood nodded. "The past won't remain buried any longer."

Outside, the gathering storm mirrored the tension inside the inn. Rain tapped against the windows as the group prepared to confront Tumblebrook with the weight of its history. In the face of the town's secrets, the trio stood resolute, ready to bring light to the shadows of the past.

Chapter 21

Old Wounds Resurface

Clara sat at her desk in the Lakeside Inn's study, sunlight streaming through gauzy curtains and pooling on the cluttered surface before her. Books, maps, and papers formed precarious towers, each a testament to the relentless search for answers. The faint aroma of coffee mingled with the crisp autumn air drifting in through the open window. Clara leaned back in her chair, frustration flickering across her face as her fingers hovered above her keyboard.

"Connecting the past to the present isn't as straightforward as I'd hoped," she muttered, breaking the room's stillness. Lady Grey, perched on the windowsill, flicked her tail lazily, as though weighing Clara's words.

Clara exhaled deeply, her gaze shifting to the Carradine ledger on the desk. Its elegant script masked the chaos beneath—a tangled web of financial inconsistencies, unexplained payments, and vanished property deeds. As Clara compared the figures to digitized town records, a troubling realization crystallized.

"This isn't just about the Carradines," she murmured, her tone tinged with understanding. "It's about Tumblebrook itself. Whatever Elias tried to preserve in his art, it's tied to this town's buried history."

Lady Grey leapt gracefully onto the desk, landing beside a folded map. She nudged it forward with her paw, her amber eyes gleaming with intent.

Clara chuckled despite herself, scratching the cat's ears. "You're better at this than I am, aren't you?" Unfolding the map, her eyes lingered on a faded label: *Town Meeting Hall.* Absent from modern maps, it had been referenced in Elias's journal as a place of resistance. The phrase came back to her: *They silenced the voices here. But the art remembers.*

Her pulse quickened as she connected the dots. The meeting hall wasn't just a building; it had been a hub for those who opposed Richard Carradine's domination over Tumblebrook. Its erasure from history felt deliberate—a calculated act of suppression.

"We need to find it," Clara said, standing abruptly and gathering the map and her notebook. Lady Grey hopped to the floor, padding toward the door with quiet confidence. Clara followed, determination rekindled.

By noon, Clara, Amelia, and Dr. Westwood were gathered around the inn's dining room table. The sunlight streaming through the windows illuminated the array of documents and artifacts before them. A quiet intensity hung in the air as they worked through their findings.

"The meeting hall wasn't just a gathering place," Clara began, pointing to a sketch of the hall from Elias's journal. "It became the epicenter of resistance against Richard Carradine's control. But its history was erased—torn down, its purpose buried."

Amelia leaned forward, arms crossed as she studied the sketch. "If Richard wanted to consolidate power, silencing opposition would have been his first move. But why erase the hall so thoroughly? What else was there?"

"Margaret Cranston knew," Clara said, gesturing to a stack of letters. "She confided in Elias about the resistance's goals. Elias's journals and paintings hint at what they stood for, but the picture is incomplete. If there are remnants of the hall, they might still hold evidence of what was lost."

Dr. Westwood tapped a finger thoughtfully against his notebook. "If the hall's destruction was meant to suppress dissent, rediscovering it could reopen old wounds. Those tied to its erasure—or their descendants—might see this as a threat."

Amelia's tone sharpened. "If uncovering the truth stirs up grudges, so be it. The people of Tumblebrook deserve to know their history, no matter how uncomfortable."

Lady Grey hopped onto the table, her paw landing on Elias's sketch as if marking it for emphasis. Clara smiled faintly, scratching behind the cat's ears. "She's always a step ahead of us."

Dr. Westwood's expression turned resolute. "Then we follow the map. If Elias left markers, they'll lead us to what remains."

* * *

The search took them to an overgrown lot on the town's outskirts, guided by the coordinates in Elias's sketches. The air was crisp, the forest alive with the scent of moss and damp earth. Dense under-brush and twisting vines obscured the area, but their determination pushed them forward.

"This is it," Amelia said, crouching beside a moss-covered stone foundation. "It matches the map."

The site was reclaimed by nature, its history concealed beneath decades of growth. Lady Grey prowled the perimeter, her move-ments deliberate. Clara knelt by the foundation, brushing dirt from a carved stone. Symbols identical to those in Elias's journal appeared, faint but unmistakable.

"He left these as guides," Clara said softly. "His way of preserving the hall's memory."

Dr. Westwood scanned the area, his flashlight cutting through shadows. "If anything was hidden here, it might still be intact. Let's look for disturbed ground or concealed compartments."

Lady Grey halted near a patch of loose soil, her tail flicking. Clara knelt beside her, digging carefully until her hands hit wood. With Dr. Westwood's help, she unearthed a small crate. Inside, wrapped carefully in oilcloth, was a rolled canvas.

Amelia unfurled it with reverence, revealing a painting of the meeting hall in its prime. Townsfolk surrounded the structure, their expressions united in defiance. At the forefront stood Elias and Margaret, their gazes resolute.

"This isn't just art," Clara murmured. "It's a declaration."

Dr. Westwood pointed to an inscription in the painting's corner: *For those who believe, the truth endures.*

Amelia's voice was steady, her resolve evident. "This painting is Elias's testament—a record of what Tumblebrook once stood for. If we share this, it could remind the town of its roots."

Dr. Westwood's expression darkened slightly. "But it could also reignite tensions. Are we ready for that?"

Amelia's jaw tightened. "Elias wasn't afraid to face the truth. Neither are we."

As they returned to the Lakeside Inn, the setting sun bathed Tumblebrook in golden light. The painting, safely packed, carried with it the weight of the town's suppressed history. Back at the dining room table, Clara carefully compared the painting to Elias's journal entries, her mind racing with connections.

"This painting was meant to be found," she said. "It's the final piece of Elias's message."

Amelia nodded, her determination unwavering. "Tomorrow, we show this to the historical society. Tumblebrook's story needs to be told—fully and truthfully."

Lady Grey curled on a nearby chair, her tail draped over her paws. Her unblinking gaze seemed to hold the wisdom of someone who had seen this coming all along.

As the room quieted, the gravity of their discovery hung in the air. The painting was more than a relic; it was a reminder that even in the face of oppression, voices could rise. Now it was their turn to ensure those voices were heard.

Chapter 22

The Silent Observer

The late afternoon sunlight bathed the Lakeside Inn's dining room in a warm, golden glow. Amelia Farnsworth sat at the long wooden table, her attention locked on the newly uncovered painting before her. Vibrant colors and meticulous brushstrokes seemed to pulse with hidden energy under the sunlight, as though the painting itself guarded its secrets.

Lady Grey circled the table with feline precision, her amber eyes narrowing as she stopped at the bottom corner of the canvas. She pawed gently at the edge, her movements insistent.

"What is it, Lady Grey?" Amelia asked, leaning in, her voice calm but laced with curiosity. "Do you see something I don't?"

The cat meowed softly, flicking her tail as she leapt lightly onto the table. She padded across the painting, stopping at the same corner. This time, Amelia noticed it too—a faint texture beneath the paint.

"That's odd," she murmured. Reaching for a magnifying glass, she peered closer. The raised lines came into focus, forming a delicate, etched pattern beneath the vibrant colors. It was almost imperceptible, hidden within the canvas's surface.

Her breath caught. "Elias left another clue."

Sketching the pattern into her notebook, Amelia turned her attention to Lady Grey, who now sat beside the painting, her eyes half-closed in satisfaction.

"You've got an incredible instinct for this," Amelia said with a soft smile, scratching behind the cat's ears. "Let's see where this takes us."

When Dr. Westwood arrived, his steady presence brought an air of purpose to the room. His leather satchel was slung over one shoulder, and his eyes immediately found the etched pattern in Amelia's notebook.

"You've been busy," he remarked, setting his satchel on the table.

"Lady Grey found it," Amelia replied, nodding toward the cat, who blinked regally in acknowledgment. "There's an intricate pattern etched beneath the paint. What do you make of it?"

Dr. Westwood leaned over the table, his sharp gaze scrutinizing the delicate lines. "This isn't decorative," he said after a moment. "It's deliberate—perhaps a map or coordinates. Elias was too meticulous for this to be coincidental."

Amelia's heart quickened. "If it's a map, it could lead us to something significant. But why hide it so thoroughly?"

"Because he wasn't just preserving the truth," Dr. Westwood replied gravely. "He was protecting it."

The dining room transformed into their command center, papers and sketches spread across the table. The painting lay at the center, a striking symbol of defiance.

"These lines," Dr. Westwood said, pointing to a cluster within the etched pattern. "They resemble latitude and longitude coordinates. Elias might have been directing us to a precise location."

Amelia traced the delicate etchings with her finger. "It's extraordinary. Anyone glancing at this painting would miss it entirely."

Dr. Westwood's voice held quiet admiration. "Elias clearly intended only those willing to dig deep to uncover his message."

"What about this section?" Amelia pointed to curved lines interwoven with the coordinates. "It looks like part of a compass."

Dr. Westwood's expression brightened. "A directional marker. If combined with the coordinates, it could indicate a specific entry point—perhaps to a hidden chamber."

Amelia's mind raced. "Clara might have been right about the quarry. Elias could be leading us to a hidden site within it."

Dr. Westwood set down his magnifying glass. "If that's the case, we'll need to proceed with caution. The quarry's instability poses a serious risk."

Amelia nodded, her determination unwavering. "I'll bring Clara in. Her expertise could be the key to solving this."

Dr. Westwood smiled faintly. "Between her analysis, your intuition, and Lady Grey's instincts, we're in capable hands."

Lady Grey stretched her paw toward the etched coordinates, her amber eyes gleaming with intent. Dr. Westwood chuckled. "Even she knows we're onto something significant."

Amelia stroked the cat's fur affectionately. "Let's hope we're ready for what we find."

* * *

Their planning was interrupted by a firm knock on the door. Exchanging a cautious glance with Dr. Westwood, Amelia rose to answer it.

Standing on the porch was a tall man with a weathered face and wary eyes. His dark coat was dusted with leaves, and his stance was tense, as though he'd been traveling through the woods.

"Ms. Farnsworth," he said, his voice low and deliberate. "I need to speak with you. It's about the painting."

Amelia hesitated. "Who are you?"

"Nathaniel Grayson," he replied, glancing over his shoulder. "I'm a historian—and a friend of Elias Carradine's truth."

Dr. Westwood appeared beside Amelia, his presence solid and reassuring. "Come inside," he said. "It seems you know something we don't."

Nathaniel entered cautiously, his gaze sweeping the room before landing on the painting. Awe flickered across his face. "It's real," he murmured. "After all these years."

"What do you know about it?" Amelia asked, her tone firm.

Nathaniel approached the table, his fingers hovering over the canvas. "Elias embedded messages in his work—clues to truths he couldn't voice aloud. But those who destroyed the meeting hall are still watching. They won't want this uncovered."

"Who are they?" Dr. Westwood asked sharply.

Nathaniel withdrew a folded letter from his coat and handed it to Amelia. The paper was aged, the ink faded but legible. It bore Elias's signature.

To those who seek the truth: Beware of the silent observers. They walk among you, hiding in plain sight, working to erase what should never be forgotten.

Amelia's breath caught. "Silent observers?"

Nathaniel nodded gravely. "A group dedicated to suppressing dissent and rewriting Tumblebrook's history. Their influence has diminished, but their secrets remain dangerous."

"Are we being watched now?" Dr. Westwood asked.

Nathaniel's gaze shifted to the window. "I wouldn't rule it out. If you pursue these clues, do so quietly."

Amelia's resolve hardened. "We won't stop. Elias's story deserves to be told."

Nathaniel studied her intently before nodding. "Be prepared for what you uncover. The truth carries a price."

That night, as the inn grew quiet, Amelia lingered in the dining room. The painting lay before her, its secrets whispering of the past. Lady Grey jumped onto the table, curling beside the notebook filled with sketches and notes.

"You've guided us this far," Amelia said softly, stroking the cat's fur. "We're close now."

Lady Grey purred, her amber eyes luminous in the dim light. As Amelia traced the etched coordinates again, the weight of history pressed against her. The truth was within reach, and though danger lurked, she felt certain they couldn't turn back now.

Chapter 23

An Enigmatic Clue

The morning sun filtered through the frosted windows of the Lakeside Inn, bathing the dining room in a gentle golden light. Dr. Westwood sat at the head of the table, surrounded by letters, sketches, and maps arranged in a controlled chaos. Across from him, Clara leaned forward, her glasses perched low on her nose as she studied a particularly faded document. The room hummed with quiet determination—the kind of tension that builds when the pieces of a long-hidden puzzle are starting to align.

"This marking," Dr. Westwood said, tapping a corner of a sketch, "appears in multiple pieces. It's not decorative—it's intentional."

Clara adjusted her glasses and examined the mark: an elegant intertwining of the letters *V* and *H*. "It looks like a monogram, but it doesn't match Elias's initials. Could it belong to someone he worked with?"

"Or against," Dr. Westwood suggested, his tone darkening. "If this represents a rival, it could explain certain gaps in Elias's records—especially if their conflict was significant enough to warrant secrecy."

Lady Grey, perched on the windowsill, let out a soft trill. She stretched luxuriously before leaping onto the table. Circling the documents, she paused at a folded letter, nudging it toward Clara with a deliberate paw.

Clara unfolded the letter and scanned its elegant script. "This mentions a 'shadowed force' opposing Elias. The tone is cryptic, but there's a hint of remorse. Whoever wrote this wasn't just condemning Elias—they were conflicted about their role in undermining him."

Dr. Westwood took the letter, his eyes narrowing as he read. "'The truth must outlive us, even if it costs us dearly.' If this was written by Elias's rival, it suggests they had doubts about their actions."

"A rival with a conscience," Clara murmured, her pencil hovering over her notebook. "Maybe they left behind these symbols as a way to ensure their story was eventually uncovered."

Dr. Westwood nodded. "If this rival had connections to the group Nathaniel mentioned, we're not just piecing together Elias's legacy— we're uncovering theirs, too."

* * *

At the Tumblebrook Historical Society, Clara and Dr. Westwood sifted through dusty ledgers under the watchful eye of Mrs. Hargrove, who hovered nearby with a mix of curiosity and exasperation.

"You're nothing if not thorough," she remarked, pulling a volume from the highest shelf. "This one documents disputes and partnerships among Tumblebrook's artisans. If there was a rival, they might be in here."

Clara and Dr. Westwood combed through the ledger's yellowed pages until Clara's sharp intake of breath broke the silence.

"Here," she said, pointing to an entry. "Vincent Hawthorne. He had an unresolved dispute with Elias over commissions. Shortly after, his name vanished from the records."

Dr. Westwood frowned. "If Hawthorne disappeared, it might not have been voluntary. This sounds like more than professional jealousy."

Clara nodded. "If someone silenced him, it might have been to protect the group suppressing Elias—or to cover up a deeper conspiracy."

Their next stop was the Tumblebrook Library, where librarian Margot helped them locate a slim file on Vincent Hawthorne. As Clara and Dr. Westwood sorted through the papers, a troubling pattern emerged.

"Hawthorne was an artist, like Elias," Clara said, holding up a photograph of one of his works. "His style is similar, but it feels sharper—like he was trying to outdo Elias."

Dr. Westwood studied the photograph. "This wasn't imitation. It's rebuttal. Hawthorne's work seems to directly challenge Elias's."

Clara held up a newspaper clipping detailing an exhibition where both artists displayed their work. "Critics favored Elias for his evocative storytelling. Hawthorne's technical precision was impressive, but it didn't resonate as deeply. That kind of rejection would have festered."

Dr. Westwood's tone turned somber. "If Hawthorne allied with the silent observers, he might have sought their support to erase Elias's legacy. But this letter suggests his involvement wasn't without regret."

When Clara and Dr. Westwood returned to the inn, Amelia was waiting, surrounded by sketches and maps. As they shared their findings, her expression turned serious.

"If Hawthorne played a role in suppressing Elias's work, his involvement could be pivotal," Amelia said. "But these symbols—why embed them in Elias's art?"

"Regret," Clara suggested. "Or a desire to be remembered. Hawthorne might have wanted his role acknowledged, even in the shadows."

Dr. Westwood laid out an unsigned letter from their research.

"'The Weeping Watcher shall guard the rest.' That phrase aligns with Hawthorne's apparent conflict—but what does it mean?"

Clara's eyes lit up. "There's a statue near the old church called *The Crying Angel*. No one knows its origins, but locals say it's been there for generations. What if the alias refers to that statue?"

Dr. Westwood's gaze sharpened. "If the statue marks something significant, it might be the key to the next part of the story."

Amelia's voice was firm. "Then that's where we go next. This isn't just Elias's story anymore—it's the story of everyone who tried to silence him or preserve his truth. We owe it to them to see this through."

Lady Grey leapt onto the table, nudging the sketch of the statue with her paw. Her amber eyes glinted with approval.

"Even Lady Grey agrees," Clara said with a smile.

As the team prepared for their next steps, the sense of purpose in the room solidified. Whatever secrets lay beneath the Crying Angel, they were ready to uncover them.

Chapter 24

Whispers in the Dark

Amelia Farnsworth stepped cautiously along the overgrown path snaking through the gardens of the Carradine estate, her flashlight cutting through the deepening dusk. Shadows stretched long across the wild flora, giving the once-grand grounds an eerie stillness. Lady Grey padded ahead, her steps deliberate and tail held high, glancing back occasionally as if to ensure Amelia followed.

"You're insistent tonight," Amelia murmured, pulling her coat tighter against the autumn chill. "What are you trying to show me?"

The estate was a quiet ruin, its former splendor overwhelmed by decay. The occasional rustle of leaves or hoot of an owl punctuated the silence. Ahead, the silhouette of the old artist's studio stood stark against the darkening sky, a skeletal reminder of past ambitions.

Lady Grey paused at the base of a gnarled oak tree, her paw scraping at the soil with surprising urgency. Amelia crouched beside her, shining her flashlight over the ground. A faint glint of metal caught the beam's light.

"What have we here?" Amelia whispered, brushing away the loose dirt. Her fingers found the cold edge of an iron ring embedded in the soil. She tugged experimentally, and a concealed trapdoor creaked open, releasing a waft of musty, earthy air.

"Well, Lady Grey," Amelia said, her voice tinged with awe, "you've certainly earned your title as Tumblebrook's finest detective."

Lady Grey flicked her tail in regal acknowledgment. Tightening her grip on the flashlight, Amelia descended the narrow stone steps revealed by the trapdoor, each one damp and uneven. The air grew colder as she ventured deeper into the chamber, her breath visible in the dim light.

The chamber opened into a surprisingly expansive space, its walls lined with wooden shelves crammed with dusty books, jars of unknown substances, and yellowed papers. At its center stood a large, cluttered table holding half-melted candles, a brass compass, and an unfinished painting.

Lady Grey prowled the room with a reverence that mirrored the chamber's solemnity. Amelia swept her flashlight across the far wall, revealing a series of pinned sketches. Her breath caught.

The sketches were unmistakably Elias Carradine's—hauntingly vivid, their emotional depth unparalleled. Yet these were different from his public works. The scenes depicted figures in turmoil, shadowy forms looming ominously, and cryptic symbols woven into the imagery.

"This isn't just art," Amelia murmured. "It's a warning."

She stepped closer, noting scrawled annotations in the margins. Phrases like *"betrayal among allies," "the watchers,"* and *"truth buried in darkness"* leapt out at her, hinting at a tangled web of secrets.

Lady Grey meowed softly, drawing Amelia's attention to a small wooden box beneath the table. Retrieving it, she opened the lid to reveal a bundle of letters tied with a faded ribbon. The first letter, written in Elias's unmistakable hand, sent a shiver through her.

"There are those who seek to silence me, to erase the truths I've uncovered. Vincent was once a trusted ally, but his ambition blinds him. I fear he has aligned himself with the watchers, trading integrity for influence."

Amelia's pulse quickened. Vincent Hawthorne—Elias's rival— was implicated directly. This wasn't mere artistic rivalry; it was betrayal of the deepest kind.

A faint noise broke the stillness: the soft echo of footsteps descending the stone stairs. Amelia's breath hitched. She extinguished her flashlight, plunging the room into darkness. Lady Grey pressed against her leg, tense but silent.

A low voice carried through the chamber. "So, someone's finally found it."

The beam of another flashlight swept across the room, illuminating the pinned sketches and the cluttered table. Amelia held her breath, her heart pounding in her chest.

"Elias always did have a flair for theatrics," the voice continued, its tone both amused and menacing. "But this... this is extraordinary."

Clutching the box of letters tightly, Amelia picked up a small pebble from the ground and tossed it toward the far corner. The sound drew the intruder's attention, their flashlight beam shifting away from her.

Seizing the moment, Amelia crept toward the trapdoor, Lady Grey moving silently beside her. Every step felt agonizingly slow. When she reached the stairs, she climbed out as quietly as possible, closing the trapdoor behind her with painstaking care. Only when she reached the garden's edge did she break into a run.

Back at the Lakeside Inn, Amelia secured the box of letters in a locked sideboard and collapsed into a chair, her hands trembling from the adrenaline. Lady Grey jumped onto the table, her presence calm and grounding.

"You've uncovered something extraordinary," Amelia said, stroking the cat's fur. "But this changes everything. Elias's story isn't just about art—it's about survival."

The letters revealed a chilling narrative of manipulation and control. The watchers weren't a metaphor—they were real, a shadowy group intent on suppressing dissent and controlling Tumblebrook's narrative. One letter stood out:

"Those who hide in the shadows fear the light, but their grip weakens when the truth finds its way to the surface."

Amelia's resolve hardened. "The truth will find its way," she murmured. "And we'll make sure of it."

The next morning, Clara arrived with fresh coffee and a renewed sense of purpose. "You look like you've been up all night," she said, setting a steaming mug in front of Amelia.

"I couldn't stop," Amelia admitted, recounting her discovery of the underground chamber and her narrow escape.

Clara's expression grew serious. "Do you think the intruder was one of the watchers?"

"Who else?" Amelia replied. "They knew exactly what they were looking for. And they're still out there."

Lady Grey hopped onto the table, pawing at a folded map. Clara unfolded it, her eyes narrowing as she studied the markings.

"This area here," Clara said, pointing to a wooded section near the old quarry. "Elias called it 'the shadowed refuge.' If the watchers are hiding something, it might be there."

Amelia's resolve sharpened. "Then that's where we go next."

Lady Grey let out a determined meow, her amber eyes gleaming. The road ahead was fraught with danger, but Amelia, Clara, and Lady Grey were closer than ever to unraveling the secrets Elias had fought to protect. Together, they would see it through.

Chapter 25

Concluding Lies

The sun dipped low, casting elongated shadows through the tall windows of the Lakeside Inn's dining room. The golden light bathed the clutter of documents, notes, and maps spread across the table, softening the sharp edges of the chaotic arrangement. Clara sat at the center of it all, her glasses perched on her nose, her fingers sifting through the mountain of conflicting testimonies. The cozy room held an almost oppressive tension, the weight of unraveling decades of deceit hanging in the air.

Lady Grey stretched languidly at the edge of the table, her amber eyes fixed on Clara with a glint of what could only be described as quiet encouragement. Her tail twitched in a rhythmic cadence, as if urging Clara to uncover the final truth.

Clara tapped her pencil against a notebook, muttering under her breath. "Every testimony has cracks," she said, her frustration spilling over. "And those cracks are finally lining up."

She picked up Dennis Griggs's testimony. His recounting of events leading up to the unveiling of Elias Carradine's works had been too rehearsed, too neat. Clara's gut told her something was off.

"Dennis claims he didn't know Vincent Hawthorne," Clara said aloud, flipping through her notes. She held up a fragile envelope retrieved from the Carradine estate. "But this letter from Elias mentions a 'D.G.' acting as a mediator between them."

Lady Grey meowed softly, her tail flicking in agreement.

Clara smirked. "Exactly. If Dennis was involved, why lie about it?"

She moved to Edith Cranston's testimony. Edith had painted herself as the orchestrator of the festival and the savior of Elias's legacy, but the letters and records told a different story.

"Elias left detailed instructions for the unveiling long before Edith joined the council," Clara said, jotting notes in the margin of Edith's statement. "She's trying to rewrite history to make herself look like the hero."

The dining room door opened, and soft footsteps signaled Amelia Farnsworth and Dr. Westwood's arrival. Amelia carried two steaming mugs of coffee, her expression a mix of weariness and determination. Dr. Westwood followed, his brow furrowed in thought.

"Any breakthroughs?" Amelia asked, placing a mug beside Clara.

"Plenty of cracks," Clara replied, gesturing to the sprawling notes. "Dennis and Edith are hiding something. Dennis denies knowing Hawthorne, yet there's evidence he mediated between him and Elias. Edith, meanwhile, claims the unveiling was her idea, but Elias's letters say otherwise."

Dr. Westwood pulled out a chair, his voice steady. "If they're lying, it's because they're protecting someone—or themselves."

Amelia sipped her coffee, her gaze thoughtful. "Who gains the most from distorting Elias's story? The watchers? Hawthorne? Or Dennis and Edith trying to save face?"

Clara leaned back, rubbing her temples. "Maybe all of them. The watchers wanted control. Hawthorne's rivalry might have driven him to sabotage Elias. And Dennis and Edith? They're just trying to clean up the mess."

* * *

That evening, Clara and Dr. Westwood decided to confront Dennis and Edith. Their first stop was Dennis Griggs's modest home. The archivist answered the door reluctantly, his face pale and wary.

"I don't know what else I can tell you," Dennis said, his voice tight. "I've already given my statement."

Clara stepped inside, notebook in hand. "We found evidence you mediated between Elias and Hawthorne. Why lie about it?"

Dennis stiffened, his hands fidgeting. "That was years ago," he whispered. "I didn't think it mattered anymore."

Dr. Westwood's tone was calm but probing. "It matters because it's part of the story Elias died protecting. Did you know about the watchers?"

Dennis's gaze dropped to the floor. "I heard the name. Hawthorne mentioned them once—said they were powerful, the kind of people who could 'get things done.' I thought it was just talk."

"And when you realized it wasn't?" Clara pressed.

Dennis swallowed hard. "It was too late. Hawthorne convinced me Elias was being unreasonable, that he wouldn't share credit. I thought I was helping. But it spiraled out of control."

"Did Hawthorne say what the watchers wanted?" Dr. Westwood asked.

Dennis nodded, his voice barely audible. "Control. Elias's work exposed too much. They couldn't let that happen."

* * *

Their next stop was Edith Cranston's stately home. Edith greeted them with a brittle smile, her polished exterior betraying cracks of tension.

"What brings you here?" she asked, though her tone suggested she already knew.

Clara wasted no time. "Financial records show you recovered Elias's belongings before they were 'officially' discovered. Why lie about it?"

Edith's facade wavered. "I was protecting his legacy," she said quietly. "Some truths wouldn't be appreciated by everyone."

"And the watchers?" Dr. Westwood asked. "Were you protecting Elias from them—or working with them?"

Edith hesitated, then sighed. "I wasn't working with them. But they're still out there, watching. If they controlled Elias's narrative, they'd twist it for their own gain. I couldn't let that happen."

Back at the inn, the trio gathered around the dining room table. The chaotic spread of notes and evidence now felt more like a cohesive story—a damning narrative of power, betrayal, and control.

"This is it," Clara said, tapping her notes. "The watchers' control, Hawthorne's betrayal, Dennis and Edith's complicity—it all fits."

Amelia leaned forward, her expression resolute. "And the truth Elias fought for is finally coming to light."

Dr. Westwood nodded. "The watchers' power relies on secrecy. Exposing the full truth will dismantle their control—and free Tumblebrook from their shadow."

Lady Grey purred softly, her tail flicking as if she, too, understood the gravity of their task.

Amelia placed her hand on the box of Elias's letters. "It's time to show the world what they tried to bury. The lies end here."

The room fell into a determined silence. Outside, the first stars pierced the night sky, a quiet reminder that even in the darkest moments, light endured. Together, they prepared to share the truth that had remained hidden for far too long.

Chapter 26

Unmasking Masks

The Lakeside Inn's grand parlor pulsed with quiet tension, its refined warmth masking the simmering unease that filled the room. The soft glow of the hearth danced across polished wood and leather-bound books, but even the fire's light couldn't dispel the shadow of secrets hanging over the gathering. Amelia Farnsworth stood near the mantle, her composed posture commanding attention, her eyes sharp as they swept the faces of the room's occupants.

Lady Grey perched on the arm of an overstuffed chair near the bay window, her amber eyes reflecting the flickering firelight. She was still, regal, a silent sentinel presiding over the room.

Around her, the players in Tumblebrook's tangled web had assembled. Dennis Griggs lingered near the bookshelves, his nervous fingers brushing against the spines of untouched volumes. Edith Cranston stood by the buffet table, her outward calm betrayed by the white-knuckled grip on her teacup. Clara and Dr. Westwood stood together by the doorway, their watchful expressions mirroring Amelia's own focus.

Amelia cleared her throat, and the quiet murmurs faded into

silence. All eyes turned to her as she stepped forward, her voice steady and sharp.

"Thank you for coming," she began. "As you know, the rediscovery of Elias Carradine's work has reignited interest in our town's history. But what we've uncovered isn't just about art. It's about hidden truths—truths that some of you have gone to great lengths to conceal."

Amelia turned her gaze to Dennis Griggs, who flinched as her attention landed on him. "Dennis," she said, her tone cutting through the room like a knife, "you claimed no connection to Vincent Hawthorne. But the records we've uncovered—and your own admissions—paint a different story. You mediated between Hawthorne and Elias. Why?"

Dennis's face flushed as he shifted uncomfortably. "I... I thought I was helping," he stammered. "Elias was difficult, and Hawthorne... he had influence. I didn't realize how far it would go."

"And when you did realize?" Amelia pressed, her eyes narrowing.

Dennis exhaled shakily, his shoulders sagging. "I stayed quiet," he admitted, his voice barely above a whisper. "I thought it was safer."

"For whom?" Dr. Westwood's voice was firm, his expression unrelenting. "For yourself or for Elias's legacy?"

Dennis hesitated, his gaze darting to the floor. "I didn't know how to stop him," he said finally. "Hawthorne had powerful connections. What could I have done?"

"You could have told the truth," Clara said evenly, her tone cutting through his excuses. "It's not too late."

Amelia turned to Edith Cranston, whose carefully curated calm was beginning to unravel. "Edith," Amelia said, her voice laced with quiet authority, "you've claimed ignorance of Elias's letters. But financial records show that months before their public unveiling, you paid someone to recover them. Why lie?"

Edith stiffened, her fingers tightening around her teacup. "I was protecting the town," she said, her voice brittle. "Elias's story is complex. Not everyone would understand."

"Or were you protecting the watchers?" Clara interjected, holding up a worn document. "This agenda from twenty years ago names you as a key organizer of plans to control Elias's narrative. Care to explain?"

The blood drained from Edith's face. "I didn't have a choice," she whispered, her voice trembling. "They threatened me—my career, my family..."

"Who threatened you?" Dr. Westwood asked, his tone gentle but insistent.

Edith hesitated, then spoke the name that silenced the room: "Hawthorne."

Amelia stepped forward, her voice sharp. "Vincent Hawthorne manipulated the watchers to silence Elias, didn't he? And you helped him."

Tears glistened in Edith's eyes as her composure crumbled. "I didn't know what else to do," she admitted. "Elias's work exposed the watchers' control. Hawthorne used them to protect his power."

Before Amelia could respond, the sound of shattering glass tore through the charged silence. The room froze as a figure darted out of the parlor window, vanishing into the darkness.

"Stop them!" Amelia shouted, already moving toward the door.

Clara and Dr. Westwood were close behind, their footsteps echoing through the inn. Amelia's flashlight cut through the night as they chased the intruder into the dense woods beyond the garden.

Lady Grey bounded ahead, her movements swift and purposeful, her glowing amber eyes fixed on their quarry. The moonlight fragmented through the trees, casting shifting shadows that made the forest seem alive.

"They're heading toward the old trail!" Clara called. "If they reach the ravine..."

Amelia pushed herself harder, her breath coming in sharp bursts. The figure ahead stumbled, and for a moment, the moon illuminated their face. It was someone familiar—a person whose involvement had always been a question mark.

Dr. Westwood veered left, cutting off the escape. "We've got them cornered!" he shouted.

Lady Grey let out a low, warning hiss, her presence halting the intruder in their tracks. The trio closed in, their flashlights converging to reveal their face fully. Amelia's breath hitched as recognition struck her like a physical blow.

Back in the parlor, the captured intruder sat under the scrutinizing eyes of the group. Dennis and Edith looked pale, their guilt and complicity etched across their faces. Clara and Dr. Westwood stood to either side of Amelia, their presence solid and unwavering.

Amelia faced the intruder, her voice cutting through the heavy silence. "For years, you worked in the shadows—manipulating, silencing, erasing. But the truth has a way of surfacing."

The intruder glared at her but said nothing, their defiance only fueling the room's tension.

Amelia turned to the gathered group. "This isn't just about Elias anymore. It's about the power of stories—how they've been controlled, distorted, and weaponized. The watchers sought to control our past, but tonight, we reclaim it."

Lady Grey leapt onto her perch by the window, her amber eyes glowing with quiet triumph.

"The truth," Amelia continued, her voice unwavering, "is no longer theirs to bury."

The room erupted in murmurs as the weight of the evening settled. The fight for Elias's legacy wasn't over, but the tide had turned. The masks of lies had fallen, and the truth was finally beginning to shine through.

Chapter 27

A Race Against Time

The town square bustled with life on the final day of the Tumblebrook Fall Festival. Vendors called out to passersby, their tables adorned with vibrant autumn produce, hand-knit scarves, and jars of golden honey. The mingling scents of cinnamon, roasted chestnuts, and pine needles lent the air an almost festive cheer. Yet beneath the surface, an undercurrent of unease rippled—a tension perceptible only to those entangled in the unfolding mystery.

Dr. Westwood strode briskly along the lakeside path, his thoughts churning. The crisp morning air carried a hint of frost, and the shimmering water reflected the pale light of the rising sun. Despite the tranquil scene, the weight of unanswered questions pressed heavily on him: the forged paintings, Edith Cranston's role in the conspiracy, and the watchers' insidious influence.

A faint rustling in the brush caught his attention. He stopped, scanning the area. From the undergrowth emerged Lady Grey, her sleek fur catching the morning light. Her amber eyes fixed on him, unblinking, as she padded forward with purpose.

Dr. Westwood crouched, his lips curving into a faint smile. "You always seem to know when I need direction," he murmured.

The cat flicked her tail and turned toward a narrower path leading away from the main festival grounds. She paused, looking back at him as if to say, *Come along.*

"Lead on, then," Dr. Westwood said, rising to follow.

Lady Grey led him through a maze of vendor tents to a quiet, secluded clearing bordered by overgrown shrubbery. The hum of festival activity faded into the background as they approached a stack of weathered crates, partially concealed beneath a tattered canvas.

The cat stopped beside one of the crates, pawing at it insistently. Dr. Westwood pulled back the covering, revealing a collection of bundles wrapped in protective cloth. Carefully unwrapping one, he froze.

The bold brushstrokes and intricate details were unmistakable—an Elias Carradine painting. But as he examined it more closely, a chill ran down his spine. Beneath the layers of paint, another signature was faintly visible: Hawthorne.

"Vincent Hawthorne," Dr. Westwood muttered, his voice tight with realization. He stared at the painting, his pulse quickening. "So this is how far you went."

Lady Grey meowed softly, drawing his attention to another crate. Inside, he found more forged paintings stacked atop a bundle of documents. Pulling out the papers, he scanned the ledgers and receipts detailing financial transactions that tied the watchers to Hawthorne. The sums were staggering, the implications damning.

"You've done it again, haven't you?" he said, scratching Lady Grey's ears. The cat purred, her amber eyes gleaming with satisfaction.

Back at The Lakeside Inn, Dr. Westwood gathered Amelia and Clara in the study. The table between them bore the forged painting, the damning ledgers, and the documents he had recovered. Tension filled the room as the significance of the discoveries sank in.

"Hawthorne wasn't just forging Elias's work," Dr. Westwood began, his voice measured but grave. "He was using it to build his reputation and undermine Elias's legacy at the same time."

Amelia's fingers traced the edge of the painting as her brow furrowed. "If Hawthorne went to such lengths, it means the watchers supported him. Elias's authenticity was a direct threat to their control."

Clara flipped through one of the ledgers, her pencil tapping against a highlighted entry. "Look at these payments," she said, holding the ledger up. "They're from the town council's discretionary fund. Only someone with access to that fund could authorize this."

A heavy silence fell over the group. Amelia's face hardened. "Edith," she said softly. "She's the only one who could've pulled this off."

Dr. Westwood stood. "Then it's time to confront her."

In the dimly lit archives beneath town hall, Dr. Westwood leaned against a desk, waiting. The musty scent of old paper mingled with the faint creak of the building settling. Edith Cranston entered moments later, her usually composed demeanor crumbling under the weight of her secrets.

"I didn't mean for it to happen this way," she said, her voice barely audible.

Dr. Westwood's expression remained stern. "Then tell me how it happened, Edith. Why fund Hawthorne? Why enable the watchers?"

She sank onto a bench, her hands trembling. "The watchers had influence. Hawthorne promised that if I cooperated, I could protect Elias's work in some capacity. But it spiraled out of control. By the time I realized what I'd done, they had me trapped."

"They didn't trap you," Dr. Westwood said sharply. "You trapped yourself the moment you chose to remain silent. You allowed Hawthorne to exploit Elias's legacy for his gain."

Tears filled Edith's eyes. "I thought I could fix it," she said, her voice breaking. "But they threatened my family, my career. I didn't know how to fight them."

Dr. Westwood's tone softened slightly. "You can still make this right. Tell the truth—publicly. Expose the watchers and Hawthorne for what they are."

Edith hesitated, her gaze darting to the floor. Finally, she nodded. "You're right. It's the only way."

* * *

As the festival's final ceremony began, Edith stood at the podium, the weight of her decision evident in the tension of her shoulders. The crowd murmured as they waited, the festive energy tempered by an unspoken sense that something significant was about to happen.

Edith gripped the edges of the podium, her knuckles white. "Thank you for being here," she began, her voice trembling. "Before we close this year's festival, there's something I must share—something that has been hidden for far too long."

The crowd stilled, their murmurs fading into expectant silence.

"I was complicit," Edith continued, her voice gaining strength. "Complicit in enabling the watchers, in allowing Vincent Hawthorne to exploit Elias Carradine's work. I thought I was protecting this town, but in reality, I betrayed it—and Elias."

Gasps rippled through the crowd, followed by whispers that grew louder as the weight of her confession settled.

"I cannot undo what I've done," Edith said, her voice breaking. "But I can ensure the truth is no longer buried. Elias Carradine's legacy belongs to Tumblebrook—not to the watchers or to anyone else."

When she finished, the silence was deafening. Then, slowly, applause began to ripple through the audience, swelling until it became a standing ovation. Edith's eyes filled with tears as she stepped back from the podium, her expression one of sorrow and relief.

Amelia, standing at the edge of the stage, exhaled deeply. "She did it," she murmured.

Dr. Westwood nodded, his gaze scanning the crowd. "The truth is out. Now the healing can begin."

Lady Grey leapt gracefully onto a nearby bench, her tail curling as she observed the scene. Her work, it seemed, was done—for now.

Chapter 28

Calculated Moves

The Lakeside Inn's parlor thrummed with intensity as Amelia Farnsworth, Clara, and Dr. Westwood sifted through the mountain of evidence strewn across the table. Ledgers, notes, and maps painted a damning picture of Elias Carradine's manipulated legacy. The deeper they delved, the more intricate the web of conspirators became, stretching far beyond what they'd originally anticipated.

Amelia leaned over her notebook, pen poised above a half-finished timeline. "Hawthorne wasn't acting alone," she said, her voice steady but laced with frustration. "He was a pawn—maybe a willing one—but still a pawn. Someone bigger orchestrated this, someone pulling the strings from the shadows."

Clara frowned, her fingers flying across her laptop. "That tracks. The North Shore Cultural Fund isn't just a shell—it's a front. Whoever's behind it wanted total control: over Elias's legacy, Hawthorne's actions, and even the watchers."

Dr. Westwood set down a stack of papers, his expression grim. "Whoever created the fund didn't just have power. They had access: to money, influence, and people willing to do their bidding."

Lady Grey, perched elegantly on the table's edge, flicked her tail and let out a soft trill. Amelia glanced at the cat, a faint smile breaking through her tension. "Even she knows we're onto something."

Before Clara could respond, the door creaked open. Dr. Westwood entered, his coat dusted with leaves. He held a slim, worn folder in one hand.

"I went back to the archives after the ceremony," he said, setting the folder on the table. "Edith's confession gave me a lead. These were buried deep—financial records and private correspondence tied to the fund."

Amelia flipped through the folder. Her eyes narrowed as she scanned the neatly typed columns. "These payments—none of them were council-approved. They're private transactions."

Clara leaned over her shoulder, studying the numbers. "The fund paid Hawthorne directly. And these amounts..." She whistled softly. "This wasn't just a side project. Someone was deeply invested in keeping him afloat."

"And that someone," Dr. Westwood said, "is still out there."

As night fell, the parlor remained brightly lit, the trio working well into the evening. The air was heavy with the weight of their discoveries, each revelation peeling back another layer of deception.

Amelia rubbed her temples. "We're close," she murmured, her voice tight with strain. "But there's still something we're missing. A piece we're not seeing."

Clara set her coffee mug on the table with a soft thud. "We've been at this for hours. Maybe we need to step back and regroup."

Amelia nodded reluctantly, stretching as she walked toward the mantel. The moment of quiet was shattered by the sound of breaking glass. Lady Grey hissed, leaping from the table to the floor.

"What was that?" Clara asked, her voice sharp.

Amelia grabbed a brass candlestick from the mantel. "Stay here," she said, her tone leaving no room for argument.

The hallway was dim, illuminated only by the faint beam of

Amelia's flashlight. Porcelain shards from a shattered vase littered the floor, glinting like ice. Among the debris lay an unmarked envelope, its edges sealed.

Amelia bent to pick it up, her pulse quickening. Lady Grey padded to her side, her ears pricked and alert. Returning to the parlor, Amelia shut the door firmly behind her.

"What is it?" Clara asked, leaning forward.

Amelia held up the envelope and pulled out the single sheet of paper. The message, typed in block letters, was chilling in its simplicity:

Stay silent, or you'll regret it.

The room fell into a tense silence. Clara's face darkened as she read over Amelia's shoulder. "They know," she said, her voice tight. "They know we're close."

Amelia's jaw clenched, her voice cutting through the unease. "Good. Let them know. We're not stopping."

The following morning, the trio gathered in the parlor with renewed determination. Clara typed furiously on her laptop while Dr. Westwood combed through archival records.

Amelia sat at the table, her focus on the financial documents. "The North Shore Cultural Fund," she said aloud, "is the key. Whoever set it up wasn't just after control—they wanted complete anonymity."

Clara's fingers froze mid-keystroke. "Got it," she said, her voice sharp with triumph. "A transfer from the fund went to an account under the name Josephine Marlowe."

Amelia's breath caught. "The Marlowes? They've been patrons of the festival for decades. Why would Josephine be involved?"

"She might not be," Clara replied. "It could be someone using her resources—someone close to her."

Dr. Westwood looked up from his notes, his eyes narrowing. "Two years ago, Josephine's estate auctioned off part of its library, including an Adler Universal 20 typewriter."

Clara's brow furrowed. "The same model used for the note."

Dr. Westwood nodded. "It didn't sell publicly, which means it likely stayed within the estate—or with someone connected to it."

Amelia's voice was firm. "If the Marlowes are tied to this, we need answers."

Lady Grey leapt onto the table, pawing at the typewriter with a decisive tap. Clara smirked. "Looks like Lady Grey's with us. The Marlowes are hiding something."

* * *

The Marlowe estate loomed over the town, its imposing facade a testament to old money and unshakable influence. Inside the sunlit parlor, Josephine Marlowe greeted them with a poised smile, though her guarded eyes betrayed her unease.

"To what do I owe this unexpected visit?" she asked, gesturing for them to sit.

Dr. Westwood placed the typewriter on the table between them. "We need answers, Mrs. Marlowe. About this—and your involvement in the North Shore Cultural Fund."

Josephine's eyes flicked to the machine, her composure slipping. Her voice hardened. "I don't know what you're insinuating."

Amelia's voice cut through the tension. "The fund paid Vincent Hawthorne, enabling his forgeries and manipulation. It was used to control Elias's narrative and empower the watchers. You were at the center of it."

Josephine's carefully maintained facade cracked. "I didn't want any of this," she said quietly. "The watchers approached me decades ago. They said they'd protect the town's history, but they were lying. When Hawthorne came to me, it was too late. I was trapped."

"And the fund?" Clara pressed.

"It was a tool," Josephine admitted. "A way to funnel resources without scrutiny. I thought I was preserving history. I didn't realize I was rewriting it."

Dr. Westwood's tone was measured. "You can still make this right. But it starts with the truth."

Josephine sighed heavily, her shoulders sagging. "Then you'd better listen carefully," she said, her voice low. "Because the watchers' story doesn't end here."

Lady Grey jumped onto the table, her tail curling as if she, too, understood the gravity of the moment. The truth, once obscured, was now emerging—calculated move by calculated move.

Chapter 29

Unraveling the Past

T he late afternoon sun streamed through the tall windows of the Tumblebrook Historical Society, bathing the rows of neatly labeled shelves in golden light. Clara sat at the central research table, surrounded by town ledgers, fragile correspondence, and newspapers yellowed with age. Her laptop's soft glow illuminated her furrowed brow as she typed, her notes beginning to form the skeleton of a story long buried.

The comforting scent of aging paper filled the room, mingling with the sharp tang of varnished wood. Lady Grey, perched elegantly on a nearby chair, watched with her amber eyes, a silent sentinel to the unfolding revelations.

Clara adjusted her glasses and leaned closer to a brittle document. The faded handwriting detailed minutes from a 1935 council meeting. Her finger paused on a hastily scribbled note in the margin: **"Pending approval by the North Shore Cultural Fund."**

"There it is again," Clara muttered, her voice a mix of intrigue and exasperation. She glanced at Lady Grey, who stretched languidly, her tail flicking as if in agreement. "This fund wasn't just steering decisions recently. It's been quietly controlling this town for decades."

Clara's concentration was interrupted by the faint creak of footsteps from upstairs. Her eyes flicked toward the sound, her senses sharpening. The noise stilled, and she exhaled, returning to the files spread before her.

Among the pile, she uncovered a worn folder containing meticulous records of donations to the North Shore Cultural Fund. Her breath caught as she saw a familiar name: **Josephine Marlowe.** The Marlowe matriarch's contributions spanned decades, many marked with the vague designation "special projects."

"Special indeed," Clara murmured, her voice laced with suspicion.

Lady Grey leapt gracefully from her perch, brushing her tail against a rolled blueprint leaning against the table leg. The motion caught Clara's attention. She retrieved the blueprint, unrolling it carefully. Faded lines revealed the layout of Tumblebrook's old town hall, complete with annotated symbols marking compartments labeled "Archives" and "Private Holdings." A scribbled note near the bottom read:

"Ensure all artifacts are secured before public access."

"This must be where they kept everything," Clara whispered, her excitement tempered by a growing sense of trepidation. "Elias's evidence, the proof of their manipulation—it has to be here."

Moments later, Dr. Westwood entered, his coat draped over one arm and fresh documents in hand. His expression brightened when Clara slid the blueprint across the table.

"A breakthrough?" he asked, settling into a chair.

Clara nodded, pointing to the marked compartments. "If these weren't destroyed during the town hall's demolition, they could still contain everything we need to expose the truth."

Dr. Westwood studied the map, his brow furrowing. "Hidden compartments in a demolished building? If the contents were moved, they'd likely be in a private collection. Given the Marlowes' influence..."

"...they might be at the estate," Clara finished, her tone grim.

As they sifted through additional records, references to the North Shore Cultural Fund surfaced repeatedly. Each hinted at its pervasive influence on the council's decisions.

"This fund didn't just steer decisions," Clara said, tapping a particularly damning entry. "It controlled them outright."

Dr. Westwood nodded, his expression dark. "It's more than a financial tool—it's a mechanism for preserving power, deciding whose voices are amplified and whose are erased."

Lady Grey pawed at the corner of the table, her claws catching on the edge of a leather-bound journal buried beneath a stack of ledgers. Clara retrieved it, opening to find detailed entries written by one of the fund's early administrators. The journal cataloged transactions and cryptic notes from clandestine meetings.

One entry, dated July 14, 1942, stood out:

"The artist's demands grow tiresome. His refusal to conform jeopardizes our curated vision. Measures must be taken to ensure compliance."

Clara's heart sank. "This is it," she said, her voice thick with emotion. "Proof that Elias wasn't just an artist—they saw him as a threat."

Dr. Westwood's gaze darkened. "Carradine's independence challenged their control. They didn't just marginalize him—they systematically erased him."

As they worked into the evening, Clara and Dr. Westwood traced the fund's connections to Tumblebrook's most influential families. The Marlowe name appeared consistently, but it wasn't alone. Correspondence from the early 20th century linked other prominent families to the fund, their contributions disguised as acts of civic-minded philanthropy.

"It's like a hydra," Dr. Westwood muttered. "Cut off one head, and another takes its place. This isn't just about Elias's past—it's about the town's present power dynamics."

Clara's resolve hardened. "If we're going to expose this, we need undeniable proof—something that ties the past directly to those in power now."

Dr. Westwood's eyes lingered on the blueprint. "If those hidden compartments still exist, they might hold exactly what we need."

As they prepared to leave, Clara spotted a weathered photograph tucked into the journal's back cover. The image depicted a group of men and women standing in front of the old town hall. Among them were two familiar faces: Elias Carradine and Josephine Marlowe.

"She was part of this from the beginning," Clara murmured, her voice low. "And these other names—" she pointed to the handwritten labels on the back, "—match the families tied to the fund for generations."

Dr. Westwood leaned closer. "Generational power. Elias must have uncovered something damning."

Clara traced Elias's defiant expression in the photograph. "He knew what they were doing. And he refused to be complicit."

Her gaze returned to the blueprint. A section labeled **"Lower Archive"** caught her attention. Beneath the label was a faint note: **"Keyed Access."**

"This could still be intact," she said, her voice tinged with excitement. "If the lower levels were sealed instead of destroyed, they might still hold everything."

Dr. Westwood's expression sharpened. "If we can find those archives, we'll have the proof we need."

Lady Grey let out a sharp chirp, her tail curling with determination.

Clara smiled, placing her hand firmly on the blueprint. "Tomorrow, we find this. And we don't stop until we've uncovered everything."

Chapter 30

Gathering Storm

The morning broke over Tumblebrook under a sky heavy with impending rain. A damp stillness settled over the town, amplifying the tension hanging in the air. Standing on the front porch of the Lakeside Inn, Amelia Farnsworth cradled a steaming cup of tea, her gaze fixed on the glassy lake that mirrored the storm clouds above. The chill of the morning bit at her skin, but it was the weight of unspoken truths that sent a deeper shiver through her.

Behind her, the familiar creak of weathered floorboards signaled Clara's approach. She joined Amelia with her own mug of coffee, her cardigan pulled tightly around her shoulders as though bracing against more than just the cold.

"You couldn't sleep either," Clara remarked, her voice quiet but edged with concern.

Amelia shook her head, her eyes still on the horizon. "No. Everything is so close, but the picture still feels incomplete. There's one piece we haven't uncovered yet, and I can't stop thinking about it."

Clara nodded thoughtfully, her fingers tightening around her mug. "The final piece is always the hardest to find. But we're getting there. You've been relentless, and you're not alone in this."

Lady Grey emerged from the garden, her sleek fur darkened by the damp air. She leapt gracefully onto the porch railing, her amber eyes gleaming with sharp intelligence. Her calm, deliberate movements were a sharp contrast to Amelia's restless thoughts.

"You always seem to know when something's about to happen," Amelia said, a faint smile tugging at her lips.

Lady Grey chirped in response and jumped down, padding toward the inn's entrance. The two women exchanged a glance, a shared sense of curiosity sparking between them.

"Should we follow her?" Clara asked, her tone half-joking but laced with intrigue.

"When has Lady Grey ever led us astray?" Amelia replied, setting her tea aside.

Lady Grey led them through the warm interior of the inn, her path purposeful. She paused in Amelia's private office, leaping onto the desk and pawing at an ornate drawer.

"That drawer hasn't been opened in years," Amelia murmured, her brow furrowing. "It's just old receipts and correspondence... or so I thought."

She tugged at the drawer, but it didn't budge. "It's locked. I don't even remember locking it."

Clara crouched beside her, inspecting the keyhole. "Do you have the key?"

Amelia frowned. "If I do, it's buried somewhere in this house."

Lady Grey, unimpressed by their hesitation, hopped onto a nearby bookshelf and pawed at a weathered box. The box's lid slid open, revealing a tiny brass key nestled inside.

Amelia retrieved it, her breath catching. "Could this be it?"

"Only one way to find out," Clara said, stepping aside to give her room.

The key turned smoothly in the lock, and the drawer slid open with a soft creak. Inside lay a bundle of papers tied with a faded ribbon and a small, leather-bound journal. The air in the room seemed to shift as Amelia pulled them out, her hands trembling slightly.

Amelia carefully untied the ribbon and unfolded the top sheet of paper. Her voice was steady but tinged with awe as she read aloud:

"To whom it may concern,

The truth about Elias Carradine must never be lost. His final works, hidden to protect his legacy, contain evidence of the fund's manipulations. They are stored beneath the old town hall, in the compartments marked on the original blueprints."

Clara picked up the journal, her fingers brushing its worn cover. "This isn't just any journal," she murmured. "This belonged to Carradine himself."

They turned the brittle pages together, the entries charting the artist's descent from a celebrated figure to a man hunted by unseen forces. His words, penned in elegant but hurried script, revealed a mind burdened by both genius and fear.

One entry read:

"March 12, 1945: The council insists that I dedicate my next series to their vision of Tumblebrook. They disguise their demands as patronage, but I see their intentions. Art should be unbound, yet they would shackle it to their schemes. If I comply, I betray myself. If I resist... I fear the consequences."

Amelia and Clara exchanged a look, the weight of his words settling over them like the storm clouds outside. Clara flipped to another entry:

"June 20, 1945: The watchers grow bolder. My studio is no longer safe. I have hidden my most important works where they cannot reach. If you find this journal, know the truth lies beneath the town hall."

Amelia closed the journal, her jaw tight with resolve. "Elias sacrificed everything to protect his truth. We can't let his story end here."

Lady Grey stretched on the desk, her eyes half-closed but her presence grounding. Clara chuckled softly. "She always knows."

When Dr. Westwood arrived at the inn, the rain had begun to fall in steady sheets, creating rivulets that raced down the windows. He stepped into the warmth of the parlor, his coat glistening with moisture, and greeted Amelia and Clara with a nod of urgency. Lady Grey perched on the arm of a chair, watching him with her usual calm intensity.

"What did you find?" he asked, shaking the rain from his coat and setting his briefcase down.

Amelia handed him the journal and the letter they'd uncovered. "This. It's Carradine's personal journal, along with a letter confirming that his works and the evidence he gathered are hidden in the compartments beneath the old town hall."

Dr. Westwood's expression shifted as he flipped through the journal. Each entry seemed to deepen the significance of their mission.

"This changes everything," he said, his voice tinged with awe. "If those compartments still exist, they could contain not just Carradine's works but the final proof we need to expose the fund's corruption."

Clara leaned forward, her elbows on the table. "The festival ends tomorrow. If anyone catches wind of this, they'll try to destroy what's left. We need to move quickly."

Dr. Westwood nodded. "Agreed. I've traced connections between the fund and the Marlowes. If the compartments were tampered with, there's a chance some of the contents are at the Marlowe estate."

Amelia's jaw tightened. "Then we need to act before anyone else does. This storm isn't just outside; it's inside the town, and it's reaching its peak."

Lady Grey let out a soft chirp, as if agreeing with the sentiment.

Dr. Westwood looked at the cat and allowed a rare smile. "Your instincts have been uncanny, Lady Grey. Let's hope they hold steady."

As the trio finalized their plans, the atmosphere in the room grew electric with anticipation. Each of them understood the risks, but the stakes had never been higher. Lady Grey, curled in her usual place by the fire, seemed unperturbed, her calm presence a quiet reassurance.

"Tomorrow," Amelia said, her voice steady. "We find the truth."

Chapter 31

The Final Confrontation

The morning rain had ceased, leaving the town of Tumblebrook damp and eerily hushed, as if holding its collective breath. Dr. Westwood stepped out of the Lakeside Inn, the crisp air biting at his cheeks. The final day of the festival brought movement and chatter to the square, but beneath the surface, a simmering tension whispered of an impending reckoning.

Behind him, Amelia Farnsworth emerged, clutching Elias Carradine's leather-bound journal tightly against her chest. Clara followed, her face set with quiet determination. Lady Grey padded beside them, her amber eyes gleaming with sharp focus, as though she understood the weight of the moment.

"This is it," Dr. Westwood said, glancing between his companions. "Once we start, there's no going back."

Amelia met his gaze, her expression resolute. "It's time, no matter the cost."

***

Together, they made their way toward the old council chamber, now repurposed as a community hall. Dr. Westwood had ensured that the key players in Tumblebrook's unfolding drama would be present—council members, festival organizers, and the town's most influential families. The chamber, with its tall arched windows and vaulted ceiling, felt imposing, the weight of its history pressing down on those who entered.

The room filled steadily, the hum of whispered conversations and the shuffle of chairs echoing off the high walls. At the front of the chamber, Amelia, Clara, and Dr. Westwood carefully arranged their evidence: ledgers, letters, blueprints, photographs, and Carradine's journal. Each artifact told a fragment of the story—one of betrayal, manipulation, and artistic defiance.

Dr. Westwood stepped forward, his voice clear and commanding. "Thank you all for coming. What we reveal today concerns not only the legacy of Elias Carradine but the integrity of Tumblebrook itself. For too long, the truth has been buried beneath layers of deceit."

The room quieted. Faces turned toward him—some curious, others uneasy, and a few laced with skepticism.

Clara joined him, holding up Carradine's journal. "This journal belonged to Elias Carradine," she said. "It documents the pressures he faced from the North Shore Cultural Fund, a group that sought to control his work and, through it, this town's narrative. Knowing his life's work held the power to expose the truth, Carradine hid his most important pieces."

A ripple of murmurs moved through the crowd. Edith Cranston and Dennis Griggs exchanged tense glances, while Josephine Marlowe, seated near the front, maintained her practiced composure despite the tension in her white-knuckled grip on the chair.

Dr. Westwood pressed forward. "Our investigation uncovered financial records, correspondence, and suppressed works—evidence tying key figures in this room to a campaign of coercion. The North Shore Cultural Fund was not a cultural benefactor. It was a mechanism for control, and its architects included Josephine Marlowe, Edith Cranston, and Dennis Griggs."

Josephine rose, her pale face set with defiance. "This is absurd," she said, her voice cutting through the murmurs. "Carradine was a brilliant artist, but he was paranoid and erratic. To claim we conspired against him is preposterous."

Clara lifted a ledger high, her tone sharp. "Is it? This ledger records payments made by the fund to suppress dissent and manipulate Carradine's career. Your name appears repeatedly as an approver of these funds."

Dennis stood abruptly, his voice trembling. "This is a witch hunt! These so-called records are circumstantial."

Amelia stepped forward, her voice calm but piercing. "Circumstantial? Carradine's own words contradict you." She opened the journal to a key entry and read aloud:

"June 20, 1945: The watchers grow bolder. They think I do not see them, but I feel their eyes, hear their whispers. My studio is no longer safe. My truth lies hidden where they cannot reach."

The tension in the room thickened as gasps and murmurs swept through the crowd.

Dr. Westwood's voice rose, steady and unrelenting. "Carradine hid his works beneath the old town hall, in secret compartments marked on the original blueprints. Those works, and the evidence they contain, will settle this once and for all."

Josephine's façade cracked, her voice trembling. "You don't understand. What we did... it was for the good of the town. To preserve its heritage."

Amelia's eyes narrowed. "Preserving heritage by erasing dissent? By silencing voices that refused to conform to your vision?"

Josephine faltered, her voice breaking. "Carradine was dangerous. He would have ruined everything we worked to build."

"No," Dr. Westwood said firmly. "He was the heart of this town's heritage. What you feared wasn't his work—it was losing control."

Guided by Carradine's blueprints, the group descended into the basement of the library—the site of the old town hall. The air was damp and cold, carrying the faint scent of stone and decay. Lady Grey moved ahead of them, her movements deliberate as she led the way.

Clara traced the faint outline of a hidden compartment in the wall. "Here," she said, her voice taut with anticipation.

With a crowbar, Dr. Westwood pried the concealed door open, revealing a small chamber untouched by time. Dust-covered crates and canvases leaned against the walls. A locked chest sat at the center, its brass fittings tarnished but intact.

Amelia knelt before the chest, her hands trembling as she inserted the key recovered from the journal's hidden drawer. The lock clicked, and the lid creaked open to reveal a trove of sketches, letters, and paintings.

Clara unwrapped one canvas carefully, revealing a haunting depiction of a lone artist at his easel, shadowy figures looming behind him. The raw emotion in the painting gripped everyone in the room, its message undeniable.

Dr. Westwood held up one of the letters. "Carradine didn't just document the fund's manipulations. He painted their crimes. This is the truth they feared."

Josephine stood frozen in the doorway, her earlier defiance replaced by disbelief. "He... he wouldn't stop," she whispered. "We tried to reason with him."

"You tried to silence him," Amelia said, her voice steady. "And now his voice is louder than ever."

The townsfolk, once divided by whispers and half-truths, murmured in unison. The evidence was undeniable. Tumblebrook's history had been shaped by deception, but the truth was now irrefutable.

Dr. Westwood turned to Josephine, his tone firm but measured. "You claimed to act for the town's good. If that's true, then you'll support restoring Carradine's legacy."

Josephine's gaze fell to the ground, her voice barely audible. "You're right. It's time."

As the crowd dispersed, the weight of revelation lingered in the air. Tumblebrook's past, rewritten for decades, now held the promise of a more honest future.

Amelia placed a hand on the chest of Carradine's works, her voice quiet but resolute. "He trusted someone would find this. He believed the truth would survive."

Lady Grey leapt gracefully onto the chest, her amber eyes gleaming with quiet satisfaction. Clara chuckled, her voice lighter than it had been in days. "She always knows."

Dr. Westwood nodded, his expression thoughtful. "The truth is out. Now, it's up to the town to decide what to do with it."

The storm had passed, but its echoes would linger, shaping Tumblebrook for years to come.

Chapter 32

Secrets Disclosed

The council chamber was thick with anticipation as Amelia Farnsworth stepped to the front, her steady gaze sweeping across the gathered townsfolk. The revelations of the library basement had rippled through Tumblebrook, culminating in this moment. The room was packed—standing room only—with faces both familiar and distant, each etched with curiosity, guilt, or unease.

Amelia placed Elias Carradine's leather-bound journal on the podium, the small act commanding immediate attention. The hum of whispered conversations stilled, replaced by a tense, expectant silence.

"Ladies and gentlemen," Amelia began, her voice firm but composed, "Tumblebrook has long prided itself on its history, culture, and people. But recent discoveries reveal a far more complicated story. For decades, this town's narrative has been controlled—not preserved—by those who sought power above all else. Today, we confront that truth."

She held up a faded letter from Carradine's journal, its edges worn with time but its message undiminished. Reading aloud, her voice carried through the chamber:

161

"To whoever finds this, know that I fought not just for my art but for the integrity of this town. My hands may be stilled, but my work will speak for itself. Justice will come, though it may take years."

Amelia's gaze rested on Josephine Marlowe, seated near the back. Once imposing, the matriarch now appeared diminished, her usual aura of control fraying at the edges. Amelia's voice cut through the silence. "Mrs. Marlowe, you claimed to act in the town's best interest. But your actions silenced voices, destroyed reputations, and buried inconvenient truths. Why?"

Josephine rose slowly, her hands gripping the back of her chair for support. Her voice trembled as she spoke. "You don't understand," she began. "The fund... it was meant to preserve our heritage, to protect what made Tumblebrook special."

"By silencing Elias Carradine?" Amelia pressed, her tone sharpening. "By suppressing artists and reshaping history to suit your version of the past?"

Josephine's composure cracked, tears streaking her cheeks as her voice faltered. "I didn't know it would go so far. I was young when I got involved—my family had always been part of the fund. It was our legacy, our duty. But somewhere along the way, it changed. It became about control, not preservation."

The room buzzed with murmurs, but Amelia shifted her focus to Dennis Griggs, whose fidgeting hands betrayed his unease. "Mr. Griggs," she continued, "you profited from these schemes. You facilitated the suppression of dissent and ensured certain families—yours included—remained at the top. Why?"

Dennis stood abruptly, his chair scraping against the floor. "I... I only did what I was told," he stammered. "Josephine and the others... they said it was for the good of the town, that we needed order."

"Order?" Amelia repeated, her voice laced with disdain. "What you really mean is control. You tarnished Carradine's reputation, destroyed his career, and rewrote this town's history in the name of 'order.'"

Clara stepped forward, holding up a ledger. "This ledger documents payments made to discredit Carradine in the press," she said, turning the page. "And this entry details bribes to council members to ensure his work was buried."

Dennis sank into his chair, his face pale and drawn.

One by one, others stood to confess their roles. Alfred Hastings, the fund's treasurer, spoke haltingly. "At first, it was small—adjustments to balance the books. But then it became about hiding payments, erasing evidence. I told myself it was harmless, but it wasn't."

Lydia Palmer, a former council member, added, "We were told that Carradine's work was too divisive, that it would tear the town apart. But looking back, I see it wasn't his art that divided us—it was our fear of it."

Finally, Gregory Leighton, a gallery owner, rose with trembling hands. "My father and I had the chance to exhibit his work," he admitted, his voice breaking. "But we were told it would be bad for business. I didn't question it then, but I should have."

The room grew heavy with shared guilt and realization.

Amelia stepped forward once more, her tone resolute yet tinged with hope. "The truth doesn't erase the pain or undo the damage," she said, "but it gives us the chance to move forward. Tumblebrook can no longer be a town built on lies. We owe it to Elias Carradine—and to ourselves—to make this right."

Nathaniel Grayson, one of the town's elder statesmen, stood slowly. "What do we do now?" he asked, his voice earnest. "How do we fix this?"

Amelia's gaze swept the room. "We start by honoring Elias's legacy. His work must be preserved and shared with the world. And we ensure that no one ever again wields power to silence or manipulate."

The council unanimously agreed to issue a formal apology—not just to the Carradine family but to the entire town. Plans were announced to establish a public gallery dedicated to Elias's work, ensuring his story could be told in full.

The festival's closing ceremony became a moment of reconciliation. On stage, members of the council expressed their regret and committed to transparency. The crowd, once fractured by whispers and suspicion, stood united in acknowledgment of the truth.

Later that evening, Amelia stood on the inn's porch, watching the lantern-lit festival grounds below. Clara and Dr. Westwood joined her, their faces marked by exhaustion but softened by relief.

"We did it," Clara said quietly. "The truth is finally out."

Amelia nodded, her gaze shifting to Lady Grey, who sat at her feet, her amber eyes gleaming with quiet satisfaction.

"It's not the end," Amelia said, her voice contemplative. "There's still healing to be done. But it's a start."

Dr. Westwood placed a reassuring hand on her shoulder. "Sometimes, a start is all we need."

As the cool night air settled over Tumblebrook, Amelia allowed herself a rare smile. The storm had passed, and though the road ahead was uncertain, it was illuminated by the enduring glow of truth.

Chapter 33

Smoothing the Shards

The morning sun rose hesitantly over Tumblebrook, its light diffused by soft clouds, as though the town itself were holding its breath. Clara walked down Main Street slowly, her footsteps echoing on the damp pavement. Remnants of the festival lingered—paper lanterns sagged on their strings, their vibrant colors muted by yesterday's rain. The scene was a reminder of celebration, but also of the storm that had shaken the town to its core.

She stopped outside the bookstore where she worked part-time. Its cheerful window display of stacked books and faux autumn leaves now felt oddly incongruous against the backdrop of recent revelations. Unlocking the door, Clara stepped inside, the familiar scent of old books and polished wood enveloping her like a balm.

Lady Grey was perched on the counter, her tail curling lazily, her amber eyes watchful. The cat's steady presence, as always, was a source of quiet reassurance.

"I know," Clara murmured, running a hand over the cat's soft fur. "There's still work to do."

The bell above the door jingled softly as Amelia entered, carrying two steaming cups of coffee. Her faint smile, though tinged with weariness, was warm. "I thought I might find you here," she said, holding out one of the cups.

Clara accepted it gratefully. "You're a lifesaver. How's the town holding up?"

Amelia leaned against the counter, her gaze distant. "Tentative. People are talking, but there's a wariness. No one's quite sure how to move forward yet."

"They will," Clara said firmly. "It'll take time, but they'll find their way."

Lady Grey leapt down from the counter, brushing against Amelia's leg before padding toward the door. Her deliberate movements carried an unspoken invitation.

Amelia chuckled softly. "It seems she has somewhere she wants us to be."

"When doesn't she?" Clara said with a faint smile. "Let's follow her."

Later that morning, Clara joined Amelia and Dr. Westwood in the town square, where a small gathering of residents had formed to discuss the festival's closing day. Conversations were subdued, the air heavy with the weight of recent revelations.

Nathaniel Grayson stood at the center, his voice carrying the authority of a man who had weathered many storms. "The festival was meant to bring us together," he said. "That hasn't changed. But we can't ignore what's happened. We have to acknowledge the truth—about Carradine, about the fund, about everything."

A murmur of agreement rippled through the group. Clara stepped forward, her voice calm but clear.

"Nathaniel's right. The festival is about more than celebration—it's about who we are as a community. That includes recognizing our mistakes. We can't undo the past, but we can learn from it and grow."

The tension in the square softened as more voices chimed in. A plan emerged: the festival would go on, but with a new centerpiece. The town hall would host an exhibit honoring Elias Carradine's legacy, showcasing his recovered works and the truth behind his story.

By late afternoon, the town hall buzzed with quiet energy as the exhibit opened its doors. Carradine's paintings lined the walls, their vibrant and haunting imagery drawing both admiration and introspection. Each piece told a story—not only of Carradine's defiance but of his belief in the power of art to illuminate the truth.

Clara stood near a painting of Main Street bathed in twilight. A young boy tugged at his mother's hand, pointing to the intricate details of the brushstrokes.

"He made our town look like magic," the boy said, his voice filled with wonder.

His mother's eyes glistened as she nodded. "Because it is magic. And he saw that when others couldn't."

Clara's throat tightened. Moments like this were a reminder of why the truth mattered—not just to correct the past, but to inspire the future.

While arranging a display, Clara noticed Edith Cranston approaching, a plate of neatly arranged cookies in hand. The older woman's movements were hesitant, her expression vulnerable.

"For you and Amelia," Edith said quietly, holding out the plate. "It's not much, but... it's a start."

Clara accepted the offering with a warm smile. "Thank you, Edith. It's more than enough."

Edith hesitated, then spoke in a tremulous voice. "I'd like to help with the exhibit. Elias deserved better than what we gave him. I know I can't change the past, but I want to make amends."

Clara placed a reassuring hand on Edith's shoulder. "That's all any of us can do. And it's more than enough."

As dusk fell, the festival reached its conclusion. Lanterns and candles cast a soft glow over the square as residents gathered for a final ceremony. Nathaniel Grayson stood at the podium, his steady voice resonating with the crowd.

"Tonight," he said, "we honor not just our history but the truths that have come to light. Tumblebrook's strength lies not in perfection but in our ability to confront our flaws and grow from them. Elias Carradine's story reminds us of who we were, who we are, and who we can become."

The ceremony ended not with applause but with a shared moment of reflection, the town unified in its commitment to a more honest future.

As the lanterns flickered like stars above the festival grounds, Clara, Amelia, and Dr. Westwood strolled back to the Lakeside Inn. Lady Grey trailed behind, her tail held high in quiet triumph.

"Do you think this will last?" Amelia asked, her voice tinged with both hope and uncertainty.

Clara smiled faintly. "It won't be easy, but nothing worthwhile ever is. The town's taken its first step. Now it's up to all of us to keep moving forward."

Dr. Westwood nodded. "They've proven they have the heart to face the truth. That's a foundation we can build on."

Lady Grey let out a soft purr, her amber eyes gleaming with satisfaction. Clara chuckled, her tension easing. "Even she thinks we're on the right track."

As they reached the inn, Clara paused, casting one last glance at the festival grounds. The path ahead would be long, but for the first time in days, she felt a quiet certainty. Tumblebrook, fractured but determined, was ready to rebuild—one truth at a time.

Chapter 34

Rebuilding Trust

The morning sun stretched tentatively over Tumblebrook, its golden light spilling across cobblestone streets and shopfronts. The remnants of the festival still lingered—lanterns swayed gently in the cool breeze, and vendors began unpacking their wares with quiet determination. On the porch of the Lakeside Inn, Amelia Farnsworth cradled a steaming cup of tea, her gaze soft as she watched children dart across the square, their laughter carrying the promise of better days ahead.

Tumblebrook felt lighter today, Amelia thought. The sunshine wasn't the only reason. It was as if the town had collectively exhaled after holding its breath for too long. The weight of buried truths had been lifted, replaced by tentative hope and the first glimmers of renewal.

Lady Grey weaved gracefully through the porch railings, her amber eyes scanning the square with an air of calm satisfaction. She leapt onto a nearby chair, settling with the poise of a sentinel.

"Ready for the next chapter, old girl?" Amelia murmured, scratching behind the cat's ears. Lady Grey purred softly, her tail flicking in approval.

For the first time in weeks, Amelia allowed herself a moment of stillness. The road to uncovering the truth had been long and fraught with challenges, but it had been worth every step. She sipped her tea, the warmth grounding her as she watched the town move forward.

* * *

Later that morning, Amelia joined Clara and Dr. Westwood in the square, their presence a familiar source of reassurance to the townsfolk. Clara was busy arranging bouquets of wildflowers at a vendor table, the vibrant blooms mirroring the cautious optimism budding throughout the community.

Nearby, Dr. Westwood spoke in low tones with Nathaniel Grayson, whose steady guidance had been pivotal during the town's reckoning. Amelia approached, her voice cutting through the soft hum of activity.

"How's everything coming together?" she asked.

Clara glanced up, her expression warm. "Better than I expected. People seem... lighter, like they've finally put down a burden they didn't realize they were carrying."

Dr. Westwood nodded. "Nathaniel and I were just discussing the Carradine gallery. The council has made it a top priority. Local artists are already being invited to help curate the space."

Amelia's heart swelled with pride. "That's exactly what Elias would have wanted—a space for truth and creativity to thrive."

Nathaniel joined them, his thoughtful expression softening. "There's still a lot of work ahead, but this is a strong beginning. And it's thanks to the three of you."

Clara smiled, glancing at Lady Grey, who had taken her place atop a nearby bench. "And her," she added with a grin. "Every great mystery needs its feline detective."

Nathaniel chuckled. "She's earned her place in Tumblebrook history."

Amelia moved through the square, chatting with vendors and

residents. She was greeted with smiles—tentative but genuine—reflecting the slow mending of fractured trust.

At the bakery stall, Edith Cranston handed out samples of her apple tarts, her sharp edges softened by recent events. Seeing Amelia approach, Edith's expression turned earnest.

"Amelia," she said, her voice tinged with gratitude. "I wanted to thank you. For everything—for helping us see what we needed to face."

Amelia met Edith's gaze warmly. "The truth was always there, Edith. It just needed the right moment—and the right people—to emerge."

Edith nodded, her eyes misting. "Still, you gave us that moment. And for that, I'm grateful."

As the sun dipped below the horizon, the festival's closing ceremony brought the town together one last time. Lanterns flickered above the crowd like stars, casting a warm glow over the square.

Nathaniel Grayson stood at the gazebo, his steady voice resonating. "Tonight, we celebrate not just our history but our courage to confront it. Tumblebrook's strength lies not in avoiding mistakes but in our ability to face them and grow stronger. Together, we build a future that honors truth and invites unity."

Applause rippled through the square, swelling as more voices joined. Amelia, standing near the edge of the crowd, felt her heart lift. This wasn't just an ending—it was a beginning, a community finding its footing after years of imbalance.

Later, Amelia, Clara, and Dr. Westwood gathered in the Lakeside Inn's cozy parlor. The fire crackled softly, filling the room with its warm glow. They sipped cider in quiet celebration, their camaraderie strengthened by everything they'd endured together.

"To Tumblebrook," Amelia said, raising her glass. "To truth, resilience, and the road ahead."

"To friends," Clara added, clinking her glass against Amelia's.

Dr. Westwood smiled, his usual seriousness softened by the moment. "And to mysteries—solved and yet to come."

Lady Grey stretched languidly by the hearth, her purring the perfect backdrop to their quiet triumph.

As they sat in companionable silence, the weight of the past few weeks began to ease. The road ahead remained uncertain, but for now, they allowed themselves this moment of peace, knowing they had helped Tumblebrook take its first steps toward healing.

Chapter 35

Semblance of Peace

The sun dipped lower over Tumblebrook, bathing the lake in hues of gold and amber. From her place on the Lakeside Inn's porch, Amelia Farnsworth cradled a warm mug of chamomile tea. The stillness of the evening mirrored the newfound calm in the town—a quiet resilience that hinted at renewal.

Below, the lake stretched out like a sheet of glass, reflecting the fiery brilliance of the twilight sky. The turbulence that had gripped Tumblebrook was finally at rest, leaving behind a community cautiously stitching itself back together.

Lady Grey appeared at Amelia's side, her sleek fur catching the fading sunlight. With the grace of a queen, she leapt onto the porch railing, releasing a soft, approving chirp.

"You've been my steadfast companion through all of this," Amelia murmured, running a hand along the cat's back. "I couldn't have done it without you."

Lady Grey's purr rumbled in response, her amber eyes fixed on the lake as though surveying a kingdom now at peace.

The weeks since the festival's closing ceremony had been a blur of activity, but progress was undeniable. Tumblebrook had taken its first tentative steps toward healing, with Elias Carradine's rediscovered legacy serving as both a salve and a rallying cry.

The newly opened Carradine gallery had quickly become a cornerstone of the town's efforts to move forward. Its walls, adorned with Elias's vibrant and evocative works, drew visitors eager to understand his vision and the story that had nearly been silenced.

Clara had been instrumental in curating the gallery, her sharp eye ensuring each piece was displayed with intention. She wove a narrative of resilience, one that honored not just Elias but the town that had finally embraced him.

Dr. Westwood had lent his expertise, crafting detailed descriptions and timelines that contextualized Elias's art within the broader history of Tumblebrook. His passion for accuracy breathed life into the exhibit, giving visitors a deeper understanding of the forces that had shaped the artist's journey.

Amelia's role had been quieter but no less impactful. She became a confidant for townsfolk grappling with the weight of their shared history. Over cups of tea and heartfelt conversations, she fostered a sense of hope that rippled through the community.

* * *

One evening, as the trio gathered in the inn's parlor, Clara leaned back in her chair, a glass of wine in hand. "It's strange to think about where we started," she said. "The town felt so fractured, but now it seems... lighter. Like we've all exhaled at once."

Dr. Westwood nodded thoughtfully, his fingers tracing the rim of his glass. "Healing is rarely linear, but Tumblebrook has shown remarkable resilience. This isn't just about recovering from the past—it's about learning to build something new."

Amelia smiled softly, her gaze flicking to the hearth where Lady Grey was curled in a tight ball. "It's incredible what can happen when people come together. For so long, this town was defined by fear and secrets. Now, it feels like we're starting to trust each other again."

Clara raised her glass with a grin. "And that's thanks to you, Amelia. You've been the heart of this effort."

Amelia shook her head modestly. "It wasn't just me. It was all of us. And, of course, our feline detective."

Lady Grey lifted her head briefly, letting out a soft meow before returning to her nap. The group laughed, the sound warm and unburdened.

The next morning, Amelia woke early to the inn's familiar creaks and groans. She brewed a pot of coffee, savoring its rich aroma as she stepped onto the porch. The lake, now bathed in the soft light of dawn, shimmered like a promise of fresh beginnings.

She thought of the gallery, the countless conversations, and the friendships forged in the crucible of uncovering the truth. These weren't just victories—they were the foundation of something new, something lasting.

Amelia's gaze drifted to the garden below, where fairy lights still twinkled among the hedges. The memory of festival-goers laughing and dancing there warmed her heart. It was a glimpse of what Tumblebrook could be—joyful, united, and unburdened by the shadows of its past.

Lady Grey joined her, winding gracefully around Amelia's legs before leaping onto the railing. The cat's quiet presence was a grounding force, her amber eyes gleaming with assurance.

"What do you think, my dear?" Amelia asked, stroking Lady Grey's fur. "Have we done enough?"

The cat purred in response, her gaze steady and confident. The answer was clear: they had done what they could, and it was enough.

As the sun climbed higher, casting a warm glow over the town, Amelia felt a deep sense of contentment. She didn't know what challenges lay ahead—for Tumblebrook or for herself—but she felt ready to face them.

The past had been confronted, the present was steady, and the future—though uncertain—held the promise of something brighter.

Tumblebrook had found its semblance of peace. And, for the first time in years, Amelia realized she had found hers, too.